Who
Be Dragons

By
Hal Shearon McBride, Jr.

Who
Be Dragons

Again, we come to the great law of right. The white race stood upon this undeveloped continent ready and willing to execute the Divine Injunction, to replenish the earth and subdue it. The Indian races were in the wrongful possession of a continent required by the superior right of the white man.

Charles Bryant, *History of the Great Massacre by the Souix Indians (1864)*
As cited by James Donovan
A Terrible Glory

Hal Shearon McBride, Jr.

A HISTORICAL NOVEL

Other Books by the Author

To Bear Witness: A Memoir (2009)

Published by Virtualbookworm Publishing

ISBN: 978-1-60264-476-2
Library of Congress Control Number: 2009939777

McBride, Hal (1937-)
Who Be Dragons/ Hal McBride
1. West Texas history; 2. Adobe Walls, 1874; 3. Buffalo Wallow, 1874; 4.
Amos Chapman; 5. Billy Dixon; 6. Bat Masterson; 7. Quanah Parker; 8.
Sweetwater, Texas; 9. Red River War.

<u>Dedication</u>

To Emily Ann
For fossil hunting and listening to my stories.

To "that pretty little Martin girl" and our two sons, Mike and David, and the inspiration for the back cover.

"Momma, we'll go, but you have to promise you won't let Daddy read every historical marker to us."

Principal Characters

(Native American names are in the native tongue to the extent the author could determine, while others are English translations.)

Brennan, Molly – Saloon girl working at various times through Kansas and west Texas; killed by Melvin King in Sweetwater, Texas while involved with W. B. "Bat" Masterson.

Buffalo Hump – Legendary Comanche leader.

Chapman, Amos – Prominent scout on the southwestern frontier. He was involved in the Buffalo Wallow fight with William Dixon. following the fight at Adobe Walls.

Coyote Paw – Comanche warrior at Adobe Walls. (A fictional or composite character)

Dixon, William – Well known historical figure recurring as a primary character throughout the book.

Duffy, Jim – Business man in Sweetwater, Texas.

Ekitaocup – Father of Quanah's wife, Weakeah.

Eschiti – Young mystic whose visions guided the attack on Adobe Walls.

Elder, Kate – Saloon girl and roommate of Molly Brennan in Sweetwater, Texas; later renowned as the companion of John "Doc" Holiday.

Finley, Dr. John – Field Surgeon of the 4th Calvary at Camp Sweetwater, Texas.

Fleming, Harry – Professional gambler and lawman in Sweetwater, Texas.

Hanrahan, Jim – Saloon owner and merchant at Adobe Walls and one of the primary individuals in the reconstruction of Adobe Walls.

Howeah – Friend and early companion of Quanah.

Kinney, Ma – Owner and operator of rooming house in Sweetwater, Texas. (A fictional or composite character.)

King, Melvin – Non-commissioned Officer in the 4th Calvary stationed in the Camp Sweetwater, Texas; killed by William B. "Bat" Masterson.

Lone Wolf – Highly regarded Kiowa leader who aligned with Quanah at Adobe Walls and in the Red River War that followed the Adobe Walls fight.

Lyman, Wyllys S. – Captain commanding at the 5-day siege of a train of supply wagon train on the Upper Washita River, September 1874. Brilliantly executed tactical rear-guard action secured a defensible position for the command.

Masterson, William Barclay "Bat" "Billy" – Well known historical figure recurring as a primary character throughout the book.

Mackenzie, Ranald– Officer in command of the 4th Calvary at Camp Sweetwater, Texas; renowned for his excellent performance during at the Palo Duro Canyon during the Red River War that followed the fight at Adobe Walls.

Miles, Nelson Appleton – Field commander of the force that defeated the Comanche, Southern Cheyenne and Kiowa in the Red River War (1874-75). "The Brave Peacock." Recipient of Medal of Honor for gallantry during battle of Chancellorsville, Virginia during the Civil War.

Nettie Mae – Prostitute traveling with the Scheidler brothers to Dodge City, Kansas, to obtain medical treatment. (Fictional Character)

Norton, Charley – Business man and Lady Gay Saloon owner in Sweetwater, Texas.

O'Keefe, Thomas – Owner of livery and blacksmith shop at Adobe Walls.

Olds, Hannah – Restaurant owner and operator at Adobe Walls and wife to William Olds.

Olds, William – Restaurant owner and operator at Adobe Walls, friend of Charles Rath and husband to Hannah Olds.

O'Keefe, Tommy – Blacksmith and operator of the livery at Adobe Walls.

O'Loughlin, Miles – Business man and restaurant owner in Sweetwater, Texas.

Parker, Quanah – See Quanah

Parker, Sally Ann –The wife of Peta Nocona and the mother of Quanah; white captive.

Peta Nocona – Comanche Chief, husband to Sally Ann Parker and father to Quanah.

Quanah – Well known historical figure recurring as a primary character throughout the book.

Rath, Charles – Highly successful businessman involved in all levels of the buffalo trade and one of the primary investors in the reconstruction of Adobe Walls. He was not at Adobe Walls during June of 1874.

Satanta – Kiowa Chief who spoke during the negotiation of the Treaty of Medicine Lodge in 1867 and was with Lone Wolf at the 1874 siege of "Lyman's supply train".

Scheidler, Isaac "Ike" – Freighter and German Immigrant camped near Adobe Walls.

Scheidler, Jacob "Shorty" – Freighter and German Immigrant camped near Adobe Walls.

Weakeah – wife of Quanah.

Wickersham, Bull – Well respected contract teamster working the military freight routes of Kansas, Texas and the New Mexico Territory. (A fictional or composite character.)

Table of Contents

Monuments

*I*n the panhandle of Texas, a few miles northeast of Stinnett, Texas, two stone monuments have been placed upon the prairie. Each stone testimonial provides its own truth. To this observer, one monument reflects in stone permanence the belief man can imposed his will upon the prairie; the other seems to suggest the expectation that the land will ultimately reclaim what belongs to the land.

One reads:

ADOBE WALLS BATTLE GROUND

Here on June 27, 1874, about 700 picked warriors from the Comanche, Cheyenne and Kiowa Indian Tribes were defeated by 28 brave frontiersmen.

James Hanrahan	Billy Tyler
Bat Masterson	Dutch Henry
Mike Welch	Keeler
Shepherd	Mike McCabe
Hiram Watson	Henry Lease
Billy Ogg	Frenchy
James McKinley	James Langton
Bermuda Carlile	George Eddy
William Dixon	Thomas O'Keefe
Fred Leonard	William Olds
James Campbell	Sam Smith
Edward Trevor	Andrew Johnson
Frank Brown	Ike Shadler
Harry Armatage	Shorty Shadler
Mrs. William Olds	

Erected by Panhandle Plains Historical Society

The other reads:

They Died For That Which Make Live Worth Living

INDIAN'S LIBERTY, FREEDOM, PEACE

On the Plains Which They Enjoyed For Generations

COMANCHES   CHEYENNES

Wild Horse   Chief Stone Davson
So Ta Do   Serpent Scales
Best Son In Law   Spotted Feather
Wolf Tongue   Horse Chief
Slue Foot   Coyote
Cheyenne   Stone Teeth

IN MEMORY OF THE INDIAN WARRIORS
WHO FELL IN THE BATTLE OF ADOBE WALLS
JUNE 27, 1874

Author's Note

*A*lthough I enjoyed their reading and I remain captivated with their meticulous detail, it was not David Lavender's *The Way to Western Sea* nor Stephen E. Ambrose's *Undaunted Courage* that gave rise my avid interest in the epic journey of William Clark and Meriwether Lewis.

Rather it was the historical novel *A Tale of Valor* (1960) by Vardis Fisher (1895-1968) that initially stimulated my interest in this grand expedition into the American west. I must acknowledge that I am an unabashed fan of Vardis Fisher after becoming enamored with his 1956 *Pemmican*, a historical novel centered on the fur trade and the Hudson's Bay Company, and his 1965 novel *Mountain Man* which provided the foundation for the motion picture *Jeremiah Johnson*.

The importance of the historical novel is firmly entrenched in my psyche. To produce a historical novel has long been a personal ambition, and the stories of Adobe Walls and Buffalo Wallow, although I cannot remember when I first heard the tales, have piqued my imagination for years. I hope this writing stirs the interest of at least one person and encourages that person to pursue even greater knowledge of the men and women of these events. And that individual emerges for the process intellectually enriched by their efforts.

I hope someone finds the same pleasure in the reading of *Who Be Dragons* that I found in its writing.

Hal McBride
Tulsa, Oklahoma
September 9, 2009

Part One

Sweetwater, Texas
1873

One

*M*olly Brennan was a whore. Though she found her work to be repetitious at times, Molly did not dislike her vocation. Given the nature of frontier society, she was afforded an acceptance and a status not otherwise available; certainly one well beyond that granted to her eastern counterparts.

Born partly from her innate kindness, she had an aptitude for fashioning the illusion of affection into her professional endeavors that produced a loyal clientele. Molly had learned long ago the male intellect possessed no natural immunity to protect it from the infectious allure of the female body, leaving men quite vulnerable to her pleasurable deceptions; ruses she judged to be quite harmless.

Emotionally gentle while not monetarily generous, Molly Brennan was truly a fine whore.

She had stepped outside the Lady Gay for no particular reason, sighted dust rising on the horizon and waited to see what shapes emerged from the clouds. The wagons she saw meant new guests for Sweetwater, and each carrying a potential customer. Molly ran her fingers through her hair and smoothed her dress. As with any successful businesswoman, she understood the importance of presentation; whether in Kansas City or Sweetwater.

In the early 1870s Sweetwater was a remote outpost of a town, a layover for cattle drovers and buffalo hunters, with a semi-permanent population of prospective businessmen. Men willing to make the ethical and moral accommodations required to service the needs of such a fluid population. Men who clung dearly to the hope the railroad would soon move west through Abilene, Texas, bringing them wealth and respectability.

A U.S. Cavalry cantonment, Camp Sweetwater, had provided a boost to the economy, although some privately bemoaned the fact the troopers were often the most quarrelsome of the groups, many being Irish immigrants who were enlisted directly upon their departure from the ships that brought them to the United States.

The number of saloons and dance halls grew with the arrival of the cavalry, but little else. Card games, mostly poker and faro, and hard liquor served to distract the men. But it was the women who had somehow found their way onto the arid plains, most of dubious history and in the company of gamblers, that were the most coveted of diversions.

There were few other distractions to be found on the parched and wind-blown plains of southwest Texas.

William Barclay "Billy" Masterson wrapped in a blanket poncho and covered with a small tarp which provided little comfort against a stiff north wind whose sole virtue was that it blew the dust kicked up by the wagon in front of him in the other direction, drove a U.S. Army freight wagon into Sweetwater. He was shivering cold to the bone.

Feeling he was intended for a much better fate, he cursed the wind for its evil intent, he cursed the late November cold snap, and he cursed all that he knew of west Texas.

A quick visual study of the main street yielded a glimpse of a half dozen drinking establishments, but it was the elegant Lady Gay Saloon with its adjacent dance hall that caught his eye. All the saloons held the promise of a stove, whiskey and company, but Billy believed he deserved the likes of the Lady Gay. While this dusty, windblown settlement in the middle of nowhere was not a Kansas trail town, it held some promise.

He was glad that the army camp at the edge of Sweetwater was the end of the trip. He could collect his wages and wait for better weather to head back to Kansas.

He slowed his wagon to survey the dance hall attached to the Lady Gay as he passed. As only fate could arrange it, Miss Molly Brennan pushed open the dance hall door, shoving it into the brisk north wind, making the bottom of her dress seem to dance around her ankles. He could not believe his good fortune. Here in Sweetwater, he'd once again encountered Molly Brennan.

He first made the acquaintance of Molly last spring in Ellsworth, Kansas, and had come to fancy her in a fashion that only a 17-year-old boy in from his first buffalo hunt can admire a buxom lady of the evening several years his senior. That Miss Molly had plied her trade in the cattle towns and buffalo camps of the southern plains did not concern the infatuated boy fresh off the family farm. A lack of self-confidence having never been among his shortcomings, Billy knew that with his charms he could lure this fallen dove into at least a temporary fidelity.

A shout from behind vanquished the fantasy. "Masterson, move those damn mules 'fore my whip catches an ear!" Bull Wickersham roared, and a red-faced Billy quickened the pace of his wagon.

Bulls' impatient bass roar brought Molly's attention to the otherwise unremarkable parade of Army wagons that made their way through the town en route to Camp Sweetwater. She smiled in the direction of Billy's wagon and quickly started a retreat from the wind into the dance hall. Molly's smile was enough to convince Billy he had been sighted and remembered.

Bull touched the brim of his hat nodding toward Molly. Molly broadened her smile in acknowledgement.

The wagons parked and the mules corralled, Billy made a direct line to the paymaster's tent. The number in line was swelled by teamsters who had arrived from Fort Stockton, anxious for an evening on the town before heading on to Fort Sumner in the New Mexico Territory. Bull Wickersham, seated alongside the paymaster's table, vouched in turn for each his teamsters. The paymaster would pay Bull for each wagon load delivered, and then Bull would in turn pay his man the agreed upon wage.

Bull's reputation was for great honesty and fairness. It was not a reputation enjoyed by most Army freight contractors. Nonetheless, when it came his turn Billy watched the count carefully.

"Masterson, one of the men headed for Fort Sumner has took sick. Trail Boss over there needs a man. Don't pay no better'n me, but work if you want to go with 'em."

"Lot of money for work a baby gal could do." It was a disgruntled slight from the Sergeant, a career 50 cents a day regular, who stood watch from behind the paymaster.

7

"King, don't see me hirin' your like," Bull shot back. Billy smiled and rustled the change in his pocket.

The on-duty Sergeant Melvin King glared at Billy, then just snorted. He judged the boy to be soft, and soft didn't belong in the world of Melvin King. However, another truth was that Bull was a massive man in height and girth; his wind-weathered and pox-scarred face belied the more gentle soul the body housed.

Bull stepped from the tent with Billy and said, "Pay him little mind 'less he gets drunk and I'd judge right now he's sorely in want of a drink of whiskey. Man's a crazy drunk." Billy nodded, but really didn't care about any Army Sergeant.

Requiring little time for thought, Billy said, "Mr. Bull, sir, I properly thank ya for offering, but I'll stay here bit. Think I'll just to go back north as ya go, sir."

"Your call. Might be a bit though, just don't know. Understand there's still some sleepin' spots down between Norton's place and Fleming's store. Might be drafty but there's two stoves. Cheap enough ya can stay a bit. Norton's whiskey might have a touch of Sweetwater Creek in it, but it'll make a dry man plenty drunk. Secure a sleepin' spot. Lots of short timers in the streets."

Bull spewed a stream of tobacco juice, then added, "Sweetwater ain't no town to be sleeping on the street."

So that Billy understood it might be a while before he took a load back north, that this would be winter layover, Bull said, "Charley Norton's got a good place here. Honest tables and fair whiskey – he don't put as much of the creek in it as others."

He chuckled and added, "And I heard he's brought some handsome Kansas girls to work there, clean healthy girls. He sees closely to it."

Billy nodded, thinking he hadn't slept any place that wasn't drafty or on the ground since his brother Ed and he left the family and the sod house to seek the good life on the streets of Wichita.

Anyway, Billy's mind was firmly fixed upon becoming reacquainted with Miss Molly and upon securing better accommodations. Driving a wagon from Kansas to Sweetwater and sleeping in a blanket roll as near the campfire as safe gave a very high priority to obtaining a room with something resembling a bed; that was out of the wind and promised some degree of warmth.

He stepped out into the brisk night wind for the short walk to the lights of Sweetwater. A night wind on the plains could give an experienced hand doubts. At times the suspicious sounds and his fantasies about what might lurk in the unseen, gave Billy the doubts. But he'd never be one to acknowledge hearing the Elephant.

Exercising what seemed his only option, he increased his pace and moved toward the lights. He found additional motivation in allowing his thoughts to drift toward Miss Molly.

The noises of the street begin to come into earshot, vaguely reminiscent of Wichita and Ellsworth. The almost animal roar generated when boredom and alcohol bring forth a correlation between manliness and meanness, triumph and defeat, either at the card table or in the illusion of romantic conquest provided by the queens of the dance hall.

Billy's fantasy of Miss Molly now hastened his steps out of the darkness with its disquieting sounds and toward the lamps of Sweetwater.

While Sweetwater might have left things to be desired, Billy did spot a Chinese laundry with a barber on his path to Kinney's Hotel.

The hotel's accommodations were much as Bull had described. Age and disposition had taken Ma Kinney out of the dance hall business, so she opened a hostel that would meet the lowest expectations of her clientele. No one expected comfort or privacy on these edges of civilization, and Ma's place didn't disappoint them.

Billy opened the door and stepped on the packed dirt floor. The light of a large candle illuminated the dusty haze that hung in the room, giving an amber glow. Her eyes dark and sunken so deeply they seemed to be seeking the back of her skull, yet peculiarly appropriate for her rail-thin frame, Ma sat at her counter outlined by the glow of a large candle placed behind her on a plank table.

Billy gauged the dress that hung on her like it was draped over a scarecrow in a Kansas cornfield had not made the acquaintance of the Chinese laundry in a time. But her gaze was so intense the boy momentarily looked away, avoiding direct contact with those piercing eyes.

"Help ya?"

"Evenin' Ma'm. I'd be havin' a bed."

"Dime a night, four bits for the week. Ya take any troubles outside. Drover be bunkin' with ya."

With a flashy smile and quick nod, Billy agreed.

"Cash up front," Ma said with a firmness and volume that belied her slight appearance.

Billy laid out his four bits on the plank.

"No refunds. Candles," she said, then directing him with a nod of her head, "Room two on the right. Privy out back."

Billy's single head bob signaled his understanding. He picked up the candle, getting a splinter from the table that was just short of raw wood.

She chuckled as the boy sucked on his wounded finger.

"Brand new table" Her voice reflected pride and pleasure in her new wood plank table.

He lit his candle from the large candle on the wood table.

The stove was at the front of long hallway, and it looked new enough for Billy to consider it luxurious. The accommodations blocked the wind, but offered little protection from the dust the wind carried as a river carries silt.

Beyond some degree of refuge, the flat timber beds were off the floor and covered with something that resembled a mattress.

He placed his blanket roll at the top of the bed and stretched out for a moment. This moment's rest became a deep all-night sleep. As dangerous a place as Sweetwater could be, Billy felt secure. He never felt safe sleeping on the open plains. His discomfort was not a fear of the Elephant. It was as uncomplicated as the lights and noises of the towns provided him a more natural and comfortable environment.

It was the snoring of the drover who had stumbled in during the night that finally aroused Billy from his sleep. Rays of sunlight crept through the cracks in the walls, the skies had cleared, but the ever present dust particles could be seen dancing in the sunlight. Billy's thoughts turned to food eaten while seated at a table, and to Molly Brennan.

Then, his vanity took reign. He found Ma still in her chair. He inquired as to "bath and barber".

"The Chinaman got a laundry. Water'll be hot, extra dime will get you clean water and he'll cut your hair suitable enough," she told him. "Ya do look in need of both." A smile cracked her face, and then quickly passed.

Billy got his clean water bath. The warm water for a moment soothed him, and not for the first time he swore that someday he'd live in a place that he could bathe a couple of times a week without it being timed.

He relaxed into the tub, not bothered by the sounds of the women on the other side of a draped blanket doing laundry. Then the broken English of the Chinaman interrupted his fantasy. "Teny up – you out now. Cut hairy."

With Billy's face soaked and lathered, the Chinaman proved to be as skillful with the razor as advertised, so skillful that Billy found it briefly disquieting. But the result was a precise shave as good as any he'd had in Kansas, not that he yet required a frequent shave. As Ma had predicted, the haircut was suitable.

He felt proper for presentation to Sweetwater society, and for an encounter with Miss Molly Brennan.

He was disappointed he didn't find Molly taking her breakfast at Miles O'Loughlin's restaurant. It was fine dining by Sweetwater standards. The beefsteak, biscuits and eggs were well to his liking. Still, he drank his fill of post-meal coffee. While not Kansas quality, the coffee was considerably better than Bull had outfitted for the long trail south, but then again Billy was slow to warm up to the trail brew.

As he finished the final drink for the tin cup, he renewed his vow to someday have the finer things, although he frankly had no idea what the finer things might be. Then, full of food, coffee and himself, he stepped outside and weaved his way across the deeply rutted streets of Sweetwater toward the Lady Gay.

Two

*T*he military past of Sergeant Melvin King was rumored around Sweetwater to be a checkered one. One fellow trooper swore that he knew King by another name during Reconstruction in Georgia and said King just escaped court-martial for the murder and dismemberment of two new freedmen who objected to his use of their dog for target practice.

His barrel-chested 5'6" frame and full mustache never concealed the cold probing steel blue eyes that lay just beneath his bushy eyebrows, a gaze that made it clear he'd harm you just for the pleasure of it. The citizens of Sweetwater had personal knowledge of his drunken fracases and his ill-tempered outbursts. They had no desire to test his reported willingness to settle a dispute with his revolver while in one of his drunken states.

However, his fellow troopers in the 4th Cavalry had a vested interest in seeing that the Sergeant was alive, well and available for duty. They only cared that he was capable and courageous in the field against the Comanche, the Cheyenne and the Kiowa. He had risen back to the rank of Sergeant during the recent action against the Comanches at Palo Duro Canyon.

The sheer, raw pleasure he took in mutilating the dead Comanches troubled even some of the more hardened troopers, but he was their shield against the hostiles.

While the troopers depended on their comrade in the field, they shunned the company of this brawling braggart of a man during the brief leaves into whatever remote settlement happened to be near their posting. Although avoiding his company in more civilized settings, they had no desire to go on a patrol or an escort assignment without Sergeant Melvin King. He kept them alive at times and they knew it.

Sergeant King, on the backside of a night of whiskey and poor luck at the faro table was departing Charlie Norton's Lady Gay as Billy, fed, fresh and smelling of the Chinaman's bay rum, made his way toward the entrance. King lurched out the door, just missing Billy on his way to street.

Amazingly recognizing the boy through his alcohol-glazed eyes, King said, "Hell, you clean up right purty, boy."

King spewed a stream of tobacco juice toward Billy's feet. Before Billy could make a foolhardy response, a firm hand pulled him inside the doorway.

"Ya daddy got ya by the scruff, boy." The sound of King's mocking laughter didn't set well in Billy's craw. "Just had me a poke at Molly. Her is fine. Yes, just fine and dandy."

King's contempt wasn't lost on Billy, but the firm hand grabbing his shoulder saved the boy from himself.

"Come on in, boy. There's nicer folk inside." Bull Wickersham's deep bass voice came from behind Billy. "That there's trouble ya got no need of."

As was most often the case, the veteran teamster was right on both counts. While Sergeant Melvin King was a soldier's soldier in the face of the enemy, courageous virtually to a fault, he could not defeat the demons that dwelled in the bottles of the amber liquid that passed for whiskey on the frontier. His troopers knew he brought them back to camp alive from the Palo Duro and off the Llano Estacado, that vast expanse of grass where the Elephant could visit even the bravest of men. But these same troopers kept their distance as their reliable duty Sergeant became a surly and utterly bad-tempered drunk.

Bull's massive arm pointed Billy toward the bar. "Bob, give the boy a shot, then I'm goin' to get what's left of his pay," Bull said with a good-hearted chuckle.

Billy politely waved off the shot and followed Bull toward the faro table where Harry Fleming was sitting. Harry had seen Bull come in the door, Billy in tow.

"Bull, I'd be a mite careful bringin' the lad to the table," Harry observed. "I recall him in Wichita. He has something of a knack with the cards. Likely own your wagons if you ain't careful."

"As I recount, Sir, twas ya who took all but my clothes," Billy allowed, somewhat astonished and flattered that a gambler of Fleming's reputation recalled him at all.

"Ya made me skin it off ya. Most have the decency not to make me work so hard. And didn't have need of your clothes," the dapper Harry laughed. "Ya got the knack and ya don't mix whiskey with ya cards."

He motioned toward an empty chair. "Sit."

"Ya brother Ed still enforcing the law up in Kansas?" Harry inquired.

Billy just nodded in the affirmative.

Harry Fleming was a gambler by trade and disposition with the strong desire to be the law, or more precisely to have the influence being the law would bring. Harry could think of no better situation. In his mind, there was profit and security for a gambler being the only law in town.

Billy admired that Harry dressed the part, from starched white shirts to his gentleman's flock coat with vest. Clothes hung well on Harry's long and thin frame. His boots were polished to as fine a gloss as the dusty climate would allow. And considerable wiping was required to sustain such well-buffed boots, given that dust seemed to seep up through the cracks of Sweetwater's finest flooring. Still, Harry saw great promise in Sweetwater.

Billy did have the knack and after an hour of five-card stud he had two dollars of Bull's money. He felt comfortable. Lady Gay somehow gave him a sense of belonging.

Three

*W*ith a few days, under Harry's tutelage, the amiable and gregarious Billy Masterson was working a faro table for Harry Fleming and Charley Norton, whom he was growing increasingly to admire. Charley insisted on an honest faro box, which Billy liked. Billy could take a man's last nickel at the table without flinching, but the thought of being viewed as a cheat was something that his ego simply could not tolerate.

To see the slender and shined Harry standing and talking with the short round and rumbled Charley interested Billy. Charley's pants were large at the waist and long in the leg, held in place by his leather braces. It was the neat trim mustaches waxed at the tip, worn by both men that Billy aspired to. Of course at this point in time, Billy aspired to any semblance of full noteworthy facial hair.

Even if he did not treat them as if they were ladies, which most were not, Charley was an innately kind man, insistent that their customers be civil to the women he had brought from Kansas to work the Lady Gay and its dance hall. Charley knew most were farm girls, some abandoned or orphaned by the parents attempting to survive on the harsh plains and prairies, while a couple were Yankee whores who had great appeal to the soldiers. Regardless, they lined Charley's pockets, and that was the idea. Charley was a businessman.

Harry's agreement with Charley for operating the gambling in the Lady Gay was the most lucrative venture of his life. While dispensing watered whiskey didn't offend his sense of business ethics, Charley was a reliable man whose sole interest in gambling was that the games were honest and he was paid his cut in a timely fashion. But make no mistake by frontier standards Charley was as ethical man who placed great value on his word.

Despite regularly watching Molly exit the Lady Gay to the dance hall on the arm of a hide man or a soldier, Billy rationalized that she was just making a living. He knew there was much to be said for making a living.

As to Billy and his newfound profession, just being under the same roof as Molly made coming to work a pleasure.

His regulars among the buffalo hunters grew. A few he had come to know when he and his brother, Ed, had hired on as skinners just off the farm. Though they left with no desire to a return tour skinning buffalo, their hard steady work had not gone unnoticed. It was a tough job in the wretched smell of a prairie littered with carcasses swelling under a blazing summer sun. The hunters liked gambling with one of their own. Charley liked the business.

From the onset, Molly was pleased to have an admirer on a daily basis. She felt the boy was pleasant and polite, traits in short supply among her clientele. A smile, a nod or a kind greeting was the most intimate gesture to pass between them in the beginning.

As to his own creature comforts, he was now sleeping in a room by himself, a warmer room closer to the front stove at Ma Kinney's hotel, and eating eggs and beefsteak regularly at O'Loughlin's place. He had given thought to a boarding house, but then again it was moving in with Miss Molly that still struck his fancy and his fantasy.

As the amiable and enthusiastic Billy's faro table became increasingly popular, Molly became more and more curious about him. Of course, the honest box was more likely to yield amiable customers, flush with their occasional gambling winnings. And Molly was a businesswoman.

During the slower times, Molly came to stand behind Billy, allowing her hand to rest on his shoulder as they spoke.

Initially she was contented that he made no effort to place his hand on her. Then, it became such a puzzlement to her that one slow morning, she decided to satisfy her curiosity with a more direct approach.

"Billy, how can ya never come to buy a piece?" His lack of an immediate response led her to blurt out, "Seems ya should want to buy a little piece."

Billy gently grasped her hand and guided her into the chair beside him. His gaze could be considered nothing other than tender.

"Molly, I guess," Billy hesitated seeming to look for the words.

He continued. "I guess it's something I learned from my momma. If ya care about a girl, then you only take what she's free to give ya. I'd not pay you for a poke any more than I'd pay ya to sit here and visit with me. Couldn't be the same. Wouldn't be the same. It's your company that pleasures me most."

He patted her hand, and Molly became even more enthralled with the boy. Molly was as smitten as a whore hardened by cattle towns can become. She now and again would allow herself to dream the perilous romantic dreams of a much younger woman.

But a hand, a voice would always materialize, retrieving her to the harsh reality of her world. Nonetheless, such flights of fantasy were pleasant respites.

Sweetwater was beginning to look akin to paradise to Billy. A paradise filled with wintering buffalo hunters and the men of the 4th Cavalry that the United States military had deemed deserving of such a posting as Camp Sweetwater.

Four

$\mathcal{B}$illy's eyes were fixed on the sway of the dress that preceded him up the outside stairs. Molly looked back and smiled. His visible excitement tickled her. She liked this brash yet polite farm boy turned gambler. He had come a long way from Ellsworth, from the boy who wouldn't have had the two dollars it would have taken to visit her in Ellsworth, even if he was so inclined.

Molly was very aware of the gaze of the boy striding up the steps behind her, and she put little extra spring in her steps. She had come to believe that the look from men's eyes came in two forms, both of which mentally undressed her, but one provided a glimpse into pure lust and the other made her feel appreciated.

But Billy's gaze was a worshipful admiration. It made her feel special, pretty and young. She had seen his eyes follow her about the Lady Gay and the dance hall many times in the months he'd been in Sweetwater. As inevitably as the west Texas wind, the time came that Molly invited Billy to come upstairs and visit her in the room she shared with Kate Elder.

For sure she knew if looks alone could remove a woman's dress, she'd be standing on the landing with a pool of cotton about her feet. She smiled at the boy who had stopped on the stairs when she reached the landing and turned toward him.

Molly opened the door, motioning for Billy to come on up and go into the room while she knotted a scarf about the door knob, a signal so Kate would know she was entertaining. Once inside, she slid the door latch shut in the hope of ensuring a bit of solitude on this afternoon. Molly wanted to feel like a lady.

Billy stood in the middle of the room, visibly tense. Molly brushed her fingers on his back as she walked past him between the two beds in the room.

"Take your things off and toss 'em on the chair," she said. Her own words sounded harsh to her, struggling to understand the difference between an invited guest and a customer.

18

Then she turned away and reached for the buttons that closed the back of her dress. She heard the sound of the taut new leather as he unbuckled his newly acquired gun belt, hung it on the arm of the chair and strained to get his boots off. Taken with the image of herself from the staircase, she just let her loosened garment fall to the floor and stepped out of the rippled cotton.

She turned and smiled to see Billy still in his union suit. "It's okay, Bill. Take 'em off." He did. He looked up. Molly's cotton dress was gone and only a white camisole slip now covered her.

She took his hand and led him to the night table that held a pitcher of water and a small pan. His whole body tensed as she placed his hand upon her breast, and then her fingers begin to soap him. The thought that he was being checked for the visible signs of disease rather than being lovingly cleansed before going to her most private of places never entered his mind.

Satisfied, Molly led him by the hand to her bed. In a rash of modesty that startled her, she lay on the bed and covered herself with her blanket before she removed her camisole slip. It pleased her that such an emotion had somehow survived within her.

She stuck her arm from under the blanket with the slip draped from her fingers, then she slowly dropped her hand, allowing the garment to slide toward the bedside. She raised the corner of the blanket and with a big, almost girlish giggle she invited him to join her.

At the onset, Molly fell into the ritual she found to be quite familiar and unremarkable. Then, as if by some form of cognitive osmosis, she embraced Billy's fantasies as her own. A soft throaty sound, as if it was generated from deep inside her breast, reluctantly escaped her lips. It was the auditory expression of satisfaction that can only come from intimate cerebral contact.

She recognized that he was completed, but not wanting him to leave her yet, she tightly held him in place until he involuntarily slipped from her. As he rolled beside her, she threw off the covers and lay arms spread fully naked on her bed.

It was an image that completely mesmerized Billy. She saw his adoring expression and the glowing, girlish smile again covered her face.

Five

Sergeant Melvin King was less than enthralled with the recurrent vision of Molly leaving with that snot of a boy, Billy Masterson. It simmered toward a flame that he tried to douse with glasses of whiskey.

Billy adored the thought of Molly, but the Sergeant King held her in an obsessive greedy lust. He had paid her fee as often as he could since her arrival in Sweetwater. In his mind this should have given him a priority with her.

King's dislike for Billy had only intensified as the boy had settled into the culture of the Lady Gay. Billy's popularity among the hunters galled King, but then of course the hunters themselves galled him. His feelings toward the hunters were a fact that a drunken Sergeant King had often made known.

But that Molly so publicly seemed to enjoy the boy's companionship and conversation was intolerable.

King stood at the bar of the Lady Gay awaiting Molly's return. Then he would prove his masculinity to her. He drank and he waited. He drank and lost money to Harry. He drank and became angry.

As his cash supply got dangerously close to dwindling below Molly's price, he stepped back from Harry's table. Feeling cheated at the table and angered that if he was to have Molly he'd have to leave a sizeable part of his pay with Harry galled him. Cheated by cards and cheated by whiskey that couldn't get him drunk enough to cloud old memories, Sergeant Melvin King staggered out the front door and made toward Molly's room. He would right all the wrongs.

Six

As the afternoon wore on, Kate made her way to the room with a young trooper fresh in town in tow. By the second step of the stairs, she saw the scarf on the door knob. Only pausing for a second, she took the trooper by the hand and led him to the enclosure under the stairs. The trooper obediently followed. Kate dropped the remnant of a tarp and a canvas wagon cover she and Molly had rigged for just such times. It afforded an adequate degree of privacy.

"My room's busy." Kate gave her escort the direct explanation. "Ya can have a poke here."

The trooper hesitated and said, "For a dollar, I want a bed!"

Kate responded, "Well now, ya ain't seein' no bed here, now are ya. Now best ya close your yap or you'll get no coochy either."

"Six bits for this," the trooper bartered. Kate commenced to raise the canvas flaps.

"Ah, Miss Kate," the trooper muttered. Believing her serious with her intent, resigned to his circumstances, he placed the dollar in her hand.

Kate let the tarp drop and tossed laid her shawl on the smoking bench. The trooper hurriedly loosened his gallowses. Kate unbuttoned his britches and let them drop, playfully checking him for the telltale signs of disease. Satisfied, she turned toward the stairs, gathered her dress around her waist, secured a firm balancing grip on a stair, spread her legs and presented herself.

When the trooper hesitated, she made a slow rolling motion toward him with her hips and said, "Don't keep a girly waitin'." The trooper's eagerness for the undertaking at hand returned.

As the trooper's thrust became more rapid, Kate gave another wiggle of encouragement.

All the while, Kate was distracting herself looking from between the stairs toward the Lady Gay across the street from the alley. Just as the trooper's enthusiasm was intensifying, she saw an enraged Sgt. King, red-faced and completely intoxicated, stagger into the alley and look up the stairs while undoing the rawhide strap from around the hammer of his pistol.

Sgt. King paused for balance, lifted the revolver from its holster and then moved quick march toward the staircase.

"Oh, god! Oh, my god!" Kate uttered. By reflex, she attempted to move back from the frightening view of King. The trooper, mistaking her words and the backward drive of her body to be the result of passion and not terror, grabbed her hips more firmly and brought his thrusting toward a now inevitable climax. His movements drove Kate back toward the staircase.

During King's heavy-footed and unsteady advance up the staircase he was completely unaware of Kate and her companion under the stair well, but he came within a hair of crushing Kate's fingers beneath his boot, which clung to the stairs in an effort to sustain her balance given her dreadful fear and the frenzied thrusts of the impassioned soldier.

Kate's eyes tried to follow him up the stairs. She turned her head upward just as her companion heaved in his final carnal surges, driving Kate's forehead hard against a stair. She staggered back, addled but focused upon the sounds from the room above her.

Billy, having retrieved his underwear, and Molly in her slip, were sitting on the edge of the bed beside each other, passions long since spent, talking, just talking. Billy was in no hurry to depart and Molly was in no rush for him to go. They laughed together.

On the landing the profoundly alcohol-impaired Sgt. King, wobbled on one foot, gun in hand. The sound of their laughter from inside the room entered him like a thin bladed Mexican knife to the gut.

One strong kick and King removed the insubstantial door from its rawhide hinges and charged to the room, standing upon the door and leaving the rawhide hinges dangling. The sight of the partially clad pair sitting on the edge of the bed fueled his drunken rage, driving all semblance of logic from his brain, releasing his violent nature into a full destructive fury.

As he stood upon the fallen door, King unleashed a shot toward the pair. Molly collapsed back on the bed. The first shot sailed past her, clipping Billy's stomach on its way to shattering his hip as it flew out of his body. Billy lunged toward his gun.

Molly was righting herself on the bed as the second shot arrived. The second shot struck Molly squarely in her chest. She fell from the bed, collapsing onto the floor. She quivered and never moved again.

For an instant, King paused. It was as if the result of the shot, some obscure recognition he had shot Molly, seemed to stop him. The distorted reasoning that if he shot Billy she'd love him vanished for a second, then his distaste for Billy again rose to fuel his rage.

King hesitated, attempting to absorb Molly's limp form lying on the floor, the unintended victim of his acts. His pause gave Billy the opportunity to retrieve the pistol, knocking over the chair in the process. Billy rolled over, now prone on the floor, and in a fear-driven calm squeezed off a well aimed shot just as the still-enraged King renewed his charge. The shot stopped King's forward motion, then he fell forward, just missing landing on Billy.

Billy fired his second shot just inches from the fallen soldier's head, assuring whatever King's thoughts were during his lunge were his final ones in this world.

As Billy tried to get up from the floor, sliding toward Molly's limp form, the morphine of fear abandoned him and a full measure of the pain made him aware of the damage King's shot had inflicted on him. A scream of utter pain escaped him and he began to flap his arms in a futile effort to reach the door, desperate to escape the room.

The sound of gunfire caught the attention of most. Two young Mexican boys were passing through the alley. They dove under behind the draped wagon canvas to find the addled Kate, with a huge pop-knot now adorning her forehead. The trooper, uncertain as to the intent of gunfire, bumped them both as he hopped on one leg attempting to regain some state of dress, and ran.

"Go see. Go see." Kate gave her panicked plea to the boys as the tears of fear and confusion began to fill her eyes.

As the youths tentatively ascended the first couple of steps, Billy burst over the threshold of the door flaying his arms. His useless legs would not propel him beyond that point. It was then that another wave of excoriating pain seeped through the sedation of fear and drove him scrambling toward the doorway.

All coherent associations suspended by fear the sight of the blood-soaked, arm thrashing before them, one of boys screamed as he retreated, "Bate sangre! Bate! Bate!" The sight of Billy on his back, bloody and arms slapping at the air, sent the boys into a terrified flight down the steps and out of the alleyway.

"What?" Kate grabbed onto and asked of Harry Fleming, who had rushed out of the Lady Gay to the sound of the gunfire and now stood beside the rail.

"What?" Kate's clutch became firmer and her tone more desperate.

"Bat somethin'. Git out of the way," Harry's voice firmed by dread.

The gunfire had brought Duffy up from his seat at the bar in the Lady Gay and he raced closely behind Harry, catching him only as Kate and caution delayed Harry at the foot of the stairs. Duffy slapped her, loosening the vice grip Kate had on Harry's arm.

Then Harry's stride allowed him to see the landing and the flailing bloody arms of the boy. "Goda'mighty! Billy's all shot to hell!"

He raced up the stairs, gun now in hand. He stepped around Billy, prepared for whatever was inside, and stepped into the carnage.

"King's a goner," Harry said, although only Billy was there to hear his words.

It only took a quick glance to determine Molly had met a similar fate. Harry's eyes turned away and he couldn't form the words to speak it. He took a deep breath and added, "Molly too." With Duffy now near enough to hear, he struggled for more words, but none came.

Duffy, on the landing, was frozen and holding onto the rail to steady himself. This was a bloody scene even for a south plains gambler. It was Duffy whose words would pronounce Molly's death.

Kate had climbed the stairs. The sight of Billy didn't seem to faze her as she walked over him. She'd seen injured and bleeding men all her life. But when she spotted Molly, the scream welled up inside her and escaped her lips, a scream that can only be produced when a lifetime of pent-up personal pain finally spills over and out into the world.

It is a sound that pierces the ears and splinters the heart.

Seven

*H*arry Fleming stepped out onto the landing, steadied himself against the rail, and once again reached for a deep settling breath. He heard the gathering noise from the street. The shots followed by the screaming of the Mexican boys had caught the attention of most of the residents of Sweetwater. Many were now gathering in the street.

To Harry's eye, two groups with a pre-existing dislike for each other were taking shape--the buffalo hunters and the troopers from the camp. The hide hunters were tired of the inactivity of winter and ready to return to the plains. The troopers were just as anxious for them to depart, hoping their exodus would signal a drop in the price of goods and services in Sweetwater, resenting the relative abundance of ready cash the hunters seemed to have.

From his position on the staircase, Harry surveyed the street and the gathered citizenry of Sweetwater below him. He spotted George Curry. George might be slightly simple, but he could be trusted to follow directions. Now at mid-stairs, he beckoned George up and met him at the base of the stairs.

Harry's voice took on an absolute, firm and directive quality that George unquestionably recognized as conveying the gravity of the circumstances.

"George, you walk, and I mean walk, over to the Lady Gay, then go out the back door and make like a turpentined cat for the Camp. You find Colonel Mackenzie, tell him that he's got a man shot up, that all hell's fixin' to break loose 'tween the hiders and his troopers. Tell him Harry said so. And damn it, George don't you tell him King's bled out."

Realizing George's eyes were about to pop their sockets, Harry put a reassuring hand solidly on George's shoulder and said, "Just do it, boy."

George did it.

It was only now that Harry Fleming turned back to the writhing Billy and took control in the midst of the bloody chaos.

He repressed his first instinct to get Billy across the street to a room above the Lady Gay, accepting the reality that the sight of the bloody and badly wounded boy would inflame the hunters and possibly the troopers.

"Duffy, help me." As they lifted Billy's skinny frame toward the bed, a shot of pain brought Billy a welcome loss of consciousness. Harry tore a sheet and fashioned a compress against Billy's shattered hip. The hip was so bloody, Harry did not even see the entry wound to the boy's stomach.

"Stay with him." He then turned to a stoned-faced, shotgun bearing Charley Norton, who had found his way into the room.

"Charley," Harry uttered in a tone that communicated how welcome his presence was. "What the hell kept you?" Not waiting for an answer, Harry said, "No son of a bitch comes up these stairs till I say."

Charley touched Harry's shoulder and nodded.

Harry Fleming entered the room a gambler. He was exiting the room an ex post facto lawman.

If there were the right men for a situation, it was Colonel Ranald Mackenzie and the soon to be Marshall of Sweetwater, Harry Fleming.

Colonel Mackenzie prided himself as possessing the poise and polish he associated with a graduate of the United States Military Academy at West Point, Class of 1862. On the frontier, where men could become self-proclaimed practitioners of any profession, Ranald Mackenzie had rehearsed this presentation on the frontier for almost two decades. Colonel Mackenzie had become everything he presented.

Although he held the hide hunters in limited regard, he supported the prevailing government policy to vigorously promote buffalo hunting as a method of making the independent survival of Indians on the plains impossible. That meant supporting and if necessary assisting the hunters in their commercial endeavors.

On this day, posturing would avert an even bloodier evening. With two men acting roles, although by traditional eastern definitions Harry Fleming had nothing to recommend him for the role he was about to play, it was the time for which each man's unique experiences on the frontier had groomed him. But it was the practical common sense of these two men that would sustain the peace on the dusty, whiskey-soaked streets of Sweetwater.

Harry adjusted the English bowler atop his head, and then stood like a stone-faced guardian on the bottom of the staircase while Charley stood at the top with his shotgun beside his right leg, visible but not challenging.

Both understood the bluff, and knew well that an overt display of weapons would provoke one of the two groups, neither a group that took kindly to being threatened. The majority of the crowd was fueled by rumor and curiosity, alternately wanting a piece of each other and wanting to know what had really happened. Harry and Charley waited.

A trooper turned to his fellows and said, "Sgt. King's up them stairs." The troopers stirred and the hide men emitted a guttural growl. The crowd pulsed ever nearer to stairs.

Harry spoke. "Stairs are closed till the Colonel arrives with his doctor."

It was his intent to leave the impression that the camp commander was on his way and a doctor was needed by all. The information delivered in a firm, unwavering voice created an adequate amount of indecision to forestall any impulsive action. Boots again kicked and stirred the dust of the street, but no one made a move toward the staircase.

Having dismounted at the town limits, accompanied by two Sergeants, four troopers carrying a litter, and Dr. John Finley, Colonel Ranald Mackenzie arrived on the scene.

Eight

*A*s with Harry Fleming, Dr. John Finley, Captain U.S. Army and post surgeon, obtained no formal education for the position he now held. The youngest son of an affluent New Jersey family, John Finley enlisted in the Union Army in 1863 at the age of 16. He was assigned to the Medical Corp and honed his newly acquired skills at the field hospitals of the Civil War. He still carried the imprint of the experience.

He had moved from frontier posting to posting until he came to under the command of Colonel Mackenzie and there he had remained. He was now, at age 38, a grizzled veteran who bothered to shave infrequently, but would bath regularly in any available body of water, seeming to relish the bath more the colder the day.

Mackenzie knew his great skill as a field surgeon and his virtual eagerness to accompany the troop into harm's way. Like his Colonel, Captain Finley had an unqualified passion for the U.S. Cavalry. The Colonel quietly admired the Captain.

Ultimately, given the loneliness of command coupled with frontier postings, it was likely Finley's conversational dexterity and his talent at the chess table that spared the Captain the wrath that would have descended upon any other member of the command. The troops, just as they valued King's field skills, knew that Captain Finley's medical skills kept them alive. They freely excused any leniency in dress that might be extended to the doctor.

A resplendent Colonel Ranald Mackenzie and the almost slovenly Surgeon Captain John Finley marched into Sweetwater. His disapproving glare suppressed any questions from those of his command as he walked past them.

As if he were on a parade ground on the Hudson River, his stride reflected authority and confidence as he moved toward Harry. Harry did not move from his position at the base of the stairs until the Colonel stopped in the street at the edge of the entrance into the alley. Then, Harry stepped out to meet him.

There they stood in the rutted street of Sweetwater, the Colonel in his best blues with tunic and the soon to be Marshall in his bowler hat, high topped boots and frock coat, eyes locked.

Colonel Mackenzie was direct. "What have we here, Mr. Fleming?"

"King busted in on one of Mr. Norton's girls at work, she's dead and he hurt the boy she was entertaining purty bad." He paused and the Colonel didn't press. "Boy got lucky and shot King." Again, Harry paused, "Colonel Sir, King's cold gone, but I don't think this mob ought to know it now."

"Sergeant King, sir." The Colonel's back stiffened even more, "Mr. Fleming, no members of my command constitute a mob, now or ever. They will disburse when I choose to order it."

Harry replied, "My apologies to the Colonel."

Mackenzie spoke again before Harry could add a remark that might diminish his expressed regret.

"With your permission, I'll send my Surgeon up to the room. These men can assume as to the fate of Sergeant King as they wish for now."

Harry nodded. In a crisp voice, the Colonel called Dr. Finley forward.

"Captain Finley, you will assist all who are in need. You understand, all who are in need."

"Yes, Sir. All in need of aid, Sir." Surgeon Captain Finley moved quick pace up the stairs. The Captain knew and understood the drill.

Harry said, "I thank the Colonel." Then, Harry gestured toward the stairs. Their backs to the crowd, they walked at a measured pace toward the stairs.

Harry was growing into the job for which he had not yet been hired.

They stood at the base of the stairs as if talking to each other, but few words were exchanged.

Upstairs, Captain Finley, no stranger to blood and gun powder, was going about his business. His rapid triage had told him that the Sergeant and the girl were not in need of his aid.

Assisted by a nauseated and pale-faced Duffy, he quickly addressed Billy's needs with skills and precision. After cleansing the areas with alcohol, he passed an alcohol-soaked silk handkerchief through the wound, entering at the gut site and slowly retracting it through the shattered hip, hoping that the act would cleanse the path of the bullet.

Billy passed out with the pain. Duffy vomited into Molly's bedside wash basin.

Doctor Finley fixed the hip in place and sealed the entry wound with the application of a firm bandage.

Then, he took a bandage and wrapped the Sergeant's head until the fixed stare from his dead eyes were covered, took blood from the floor and gave the Sergeant the appearance of suffering from a severe head wound. He quickly took a blanket from the bed and covered the dead Sergeant's gaping chest wound. Having postured King's body in as life-like a fashion as he could, Surgeon Captain Finley stepped to the landing.

"Colonel Sir, the stretcher bearers, please. I'd recommend bringin' the wagon as near the bottom of the steps as possible."

With a wave of the Colonel's hand, Corporal Jennings, an aspiring Army surgeon, with two troopers made quick step past the somber pair and up the stairs.

Doctor Finley, hand extended, stopped them at the doorway. "Inside pay close attention only to your Sergeant. He's just hangin' in. Take him directly the medicine tent, then post guards at the flap. Jostle him and the Colonel will see ya muck horses the rest of your enlistment."

The doctor, never fancying himself a thespian, was pleased with his theatrical performance.

Dr. Finley followed the stretcher and Corporal Jennings down the stairs. As he had hoped, the troopers took King to still be among the living. He then approached the Colonel and Harry Fleming, positioning himself so that he was facing them with his back turned to the street.

Addressing only Colonel Mackenzie, he plainly stated, "King's cold dead, Sir. Couldn't have lasted more n' a minute. Will not be said 'till you say so."

Turning to Harry, he said, "The boy is gut shot and bone-busted, but he has a bit of a chance. Norton's place would likely be the best for him. No spare laudanum. Chinaman's concoction will ease the pain a tad. Jennings will look in on him in the morning."

Harry's face gave away his concern about the delay. Mackenzie spoke over him. "Mr. Fleming, it has to appear that my medical team is devoting every ounce of their energy to saving Sergeant King." He paused. "Harry, better the boy dies than we lose a dozen or so men in this street today. It is a time when a faint deception serves a greater good than the truth."

Finley inhaled deeply. "With your permission, I'll hustle that wagon along like the man's life depended on my speed."

Only now did Harry speak. "Captain Finley, I thank you."

Colonel Mackenzie said, "Mr. Fleming, it is my intention to awaken the Sergeant's troops at 4 AM. They will be dispatched on a patrol to survey the conditions around the Palo Duro. I will inform them of their Sergeant's demise at that time. Every member of Sergeant King's troops will be in the saddle by daybreak. As to your hunters, you may assume I have concerns. I will tell my command about Comanche sightings in the area. The guard will be doubled for the next few days with the order that any movement is to be considered a hostile. I expect no one from your community will approach the camp during the evening hours."

"I understand your concerns, Colonel," Harry replied, "Reports of Comanche sightings are always of concern."

"Now, Mr. Fleming, I believe it would be best for us to shake hands, and I will depart to see after my injured Sergeant."

Removing his glove, he extended his hand. They shook hands firmly enough and long enough for all to take their notice.

Nine

*A*t 4 AM the troops were awakened and assembled. Now wearing the clothing of a field commander and sitting astride his favorite horse, Colonel Ranald Mackenzie addressed the collected troops. He told them of Comanche activity in the area, delivering a firm reminder of their commitment to God and the United States of America. The chill of the morning air surrounded his words with a smoky mist, giving them added emphasis.

Listening through the open flap of the hospital tent, Doctor Finley thought to himself, there is always Comanche activity in western Texas. He admired the Colonel's domination of the English language, cloaking the commonplace in a sense of urgency.

The Colonel, continuing in his clipped and precise delivery, detailed the objectives of the patrol.

It was in closing that he told the assemblage of the death of their comrade, Sergeant Melvin King. No trooper dared twitch, much less move within the ranks.

A smile came to Finley's grizzled face as Colonel Mackenzie completed his motivational and directional address. He muttered to himself, "He mucked you, lads. He mucked ya." His smile broadened as he finished his thought. "By God, made ya feel like men in its doin'."

Turning to Lt. George Calhoun, who was to command the patrol, he handed him a folded paper and directed him, "As midday starts to find you, seek shade. Read this to the men." Then, in full voice, he said, "Lt. Calhoun, take your patrol."

The assembled troopers under the command of Lt. George Calhoun mounted and departed.

And so the death of Sergeant Melvin King was announced to a 4:30 AM assembly of the 4th Calvary on the parade grounds of Camp Sweetwater, Texas. Come afternoon, the Sergeant would be buried with full honors in the cemetery at Camp Sweetwater, Texas.

By mid-afternoon, on an arm of the Brazos River to the north of Camp Sweetwater, Lt. George Calhoun found fitting shade, a grove that was a blend of hackberry, cottonwood and mimosa. Here he gathered the men of his patrol and as ordered, he read Colonel Mackenzie's words.

"Gentlemen, know as you now hear these words, Melvin King, Sergeant of the 4th United States Cavalry, has been committed to the earth with full military honors. Sergeant King was memorialized as he was, an outstanding soldier without peer in the face of the enemy, yet possessed of man's frailties. To pay him the proper and honest respect he deserves, those of us who knew him and who have fought beside him cannot allow ourselves to forget either. Now, I respectfully request, under the leadership of Sergeant Major O'Rourke, your patrol pray the Rosary and find your personal peace with the death of your departed fellow trooper. I wish you Godspeed as you continue your mission."

Lt. Calhoun added, "Signed by Colonel Ranald Mackenzie."

So, there in a grove of trees along a branch of the Brazos River, a praying of Rosary with the Irish Catholics who filled their ranks in full voice, his men said their goodbyes to Sergeant Melvin King, a fallen comrade in a drinking man's army.

Ten

T he morning of Molly's burial broke clear, cool and crisp. Such a day came now and again in late January on the plains. The services at the grave were well enough attended.

Seeing as none of the gathering had brought a Bible, if any actually owned one, a buffalo hunter who claimed to have been a preacher in a previous life said some kind words, making a reference to a saying he claimed was Biblical, "Ain't nobody here that ain't done their share of wrong deeds in this life, so Lord let Miss Molly Brennan now enjoy her peace without undue burden. Suspect her life here was burden aplenty."

Charley Norton and Harry Fleming added a few nice words.

At Harry's instruction, Jim Duffy had stayed with Billy. Despite reassurances, Harry had concern that forgiveness was not completely forthcoming from the horse soldiers at Camp Sweetwater.

True to his word, Colonel Mackenzie had sent out a patrol departing at first light that included all Sergeant King's platoon toward the Palo Duro country. It was a dangerous enough journey that the troopers' interest in staying alive would distract them from the loss of their Sergeant. And hopefully convince them that the presence of Sergeant Melvin A. King was not required for their survival out on the Llano Estacado.

As Kate and several of girls lingered at the gravesite, Charley Norton, allowing them their grief at the loss of a mate, hung back a respectful bit. When the girls begin to move away, a couple of Mexicans, likely impatient to be done, begin to cover the grave. Charley fell into stride beside Kate, taking her arm and allowing some separation to be created.

Then he said, "Kate, I brought you girls to Sweetwater and I am sorry about Molly." Kate knowingly patted his hand.

Charley continued, "Now, Bull has three wagons haulin' supplies for Fort Griffin and he's holding them up for you right now. Lots of soldier boys, recruits and a clear deep spring there. Damn it, Kate, just better for you."

Still sensing a hesitation, he added, "And I hear that sick son of a bitch Holliday you took a fancy to is dealing down there." Then, as if regretting his words had provided Kate with that information, his tone became quieter and more serious. He said, "Kate, he's a dangerous dying man."

Kate smiled and said, "I was goin' anyways, Charley, I got to the shake the dust of this place outta my bloomers. Fort Griffin's good a place as the next." She reached out and took his hand as they walked back toward the buildings of Sweetwater.

Within the hour, Kate was ready. She stood beside the wagon and thanked Bull, adding, "Take good care of that Billy Bat now, ya hear."

Bull just nodded, turned and walked toward O'Loughlin's place. Coffee sounded good about now. Sending a whore out on the trail with his teamsters didn't sound so good.

Charley helped Kate into a wagon. Before he did, she leaned over and kissed him on the cheek and whispered to him, "Charley, you treated me good and I thank you. And Charley, out here we're all dangerous and dying."

Charley thought on it as he watched the wagons until they vanished beneath the horizon. He thought on death, on the dangerous and the dying. Addressing no one, he said aloud, "Yeah, Kate, we are. We certain as hell are."

He turned and walked back toward the Lady Gay. He stopped as a dust devil formed and passed over the street and dissipated.

Billy Bat. A smile broke Charley's face.

Eleven

*B*illy stirred in a manner that the young lady posted with him was certain was the rattle of dying man, and she did not want to witness the event, convinced that it was a bad omen as to her own future.

She had started to scoot out the door when he questioned, "Alive?" Then, as he attempted to stir, he added, "I hurt."

The girl looked at him and said, "Be praised ya feel a'tall. Ya looked awful bad." She hustled from the room to fetch Mr. Charley and Mr. Harry.

Now certainly dying was a part of living on the plains, and it did not often provoke great emotion in either Harry or Charley, but the boy was still fresh. Although they were friends and allies, neither would have grieved long at the other's death.

But both saw something of themselves in Billy, so given a choice they would prefer he lived. So on this day the harsh rule of natural order to which they otherwise adhered was suspended.

Charley got to the room first. By the time Harry arrived, Charley had both thumbs expanding out his braces like a proud father.

"Want ya to look at this. The Bat boy's done resurrected himself," Charley announced.

"So he has, Charley, so he has." The widest of smiles spread across Harry's face. "I'll send over to Miles' place. He needs nourishment."

Obviously delighted with Billy's consciousness, Charley chortled, "The boy might want a poke first." Charley laughed at his own humor.

"Feed 'em first." Harry was still smiling. Charley would swear the smile didn't leave Harry's face for two days.

Harry returned with a classic English bowler like Harry's hat that Billy so admired. "A hat to your health, boy," Harry said as he placed it on Billy's head with a firm tap of his hand on the crown.

Medical Corporal Jennings' services were secured to assure the recovery would continue.

All in all, Billy was glad to be alive. The gunshot had shattered his right hip and the limp would follow him the rest of his life.

Even in the panic of his pain, he was aware that Molly was dead on the floor of her room. But it was speaking of it now that gave it the permanence that made it real. He mourned, but it was her last hours of life that would cling to his memory and not the seconds of her death.

Billy Masterson had arrived in Sweetwater, Texas, looking at the backside of a mule, an adolescent farm boy with a vigorous desire for position, although he had no idea what position was beyond what he had seen in Wichita and Ellsworth. But he knew the settled life of a farmer was not what he wanted.

In April of 1874, he departed Sweetwater as Bat Masterson, a man with a growing reputation as the gambler who had shot and killed a quarrelsome, loud-mouthed Sergeant; a gunman with standing.

Bat Masterson was now deemed to be a man you contradicted at your own peril. He basked in the attention and frontier style respect that the events in Sweetwater brought him. It gave him a bit of the status he pursued.

To be sure shuffling in the back of one of Bull Wickersham's freighters, a daybreak exodus from Sweetwater, a bouncing, bone-jarring ride to pick up a load of buffalo hides in Adobe Walls and then on to Dodge City, was not his envisioned departure. He would have preferred a more opulent exit, but he settled for anything that took him safely away from west Texas.

During his brief stay in Sweetwater, he became educated to the importance of perception and the great power of the correctly spoken word.

The limp, a newly acquired classic English bowler hat that he especially admired and a snappy new name, a name he now embraced, begin to distinguish him. He wanted folks to know from a distance that it was Bat Masterson walking their way. These trappings all suited his ego and his purposes well enough.

Part Two

Llano Estacado
June 1874

Twelve

*T*o the observer, Dixon appeared to be moving as if he were somehow suspended in the tall grass of the prairie. The height and motion of the grass made it seem as if there was only a man and a horse swimming in a sea of grass, a sea which for the most part concealed his horse from view. The buckskin coloring of his horse enhanced the illusion, allowing the animal to fade into the shadings of the wheat colored seed tops. Dixon and the buckskin moved in fluid unison, allowing horse and rider to attain an effortless and virtually melodic harmony with the waving movement of the tall grass.

But on the Llano Estacado, this day as with most days, there were no observers.

For most men such a vast emptiness drives them into a frantic pursuit of human contact, where they can find validation by placing themselves in circumstances that require other men to hear their words, even if everyone is talking at the same time.

Billy Dixon was not such a man. The remote seclusion from the noise of human clamor brought solitude, a personal peace he had never found anywhere else.

Dixon was drawn to this land as other men, over time, have been drawn to the sea. In the almost continuous motions of the grass on this undisturbed prairie Dixon found his calming waves. In the sighting of a cottonwood oasis, with its willows and hackberry trees standing as sentinels on the shore line of a seasonally flowing creek, Dixon had his exhilarating landfalls.

The Llano was a place of which most white men knew little and spoke about only in terms of its harsh and unforgiving nature, but Dixon, now 23 years of age, found it more comforting and predictable than the logging camps along the Missouri River where he had worked after the death of his parents when he was 12.

Actually, he had come to feel as if he had been led to this place by the buffalo. This was one of the rare mystical emotions he allowed himself. This grassy sea he simply accepted and was grateful for having been allowed to discover such a place existed. A straightforward land with its subtle topography that was incredibly complex and filled with the possibility of new discovery.

He was coming to measure hiring on with a crew of buffalo hunters in Wichita at the age of 15 as having been providential. His sole aptitude for such employment had been his substantial proficiency with a long gun.

His inherent knack with a long gun had been noted by a hunter for a logging camp on the Missouri River where the 13-year-old Dixon was working as a mule tender. The hunter knew the value of a fresh-faced boy still shy of his first shave in marksmanship contests where significant side bets were placed. Dixon was an enthusiastic and apt pupil.

By the age of 16, Dixon was as lethal a hunter as there was following the herds. His skinners never wanted for work. He took great pride in the shot itself, the longer the shot the better. Beyond the unvoiced pride he took in his marksmanship and the cash, he found little pleasure in the bloody business.

And unlike his hunting companions, he was cautious with his money. While he would say, "No whorin' and no cheap whiskey", he always took advantage of the opportunity to buy a newer repeating rifle or the latest Sharps rifle. Although he recognized their usefulness, handguns held little fascination for him. Taking advantage of another man's poor financial circumstances to make such a purchase gave him no remorse. He felt that the man had placed himself in that position.

A high-quality whiskey was another tale. He could sit in the corner of an otherwise crowded room sipping a single glass of a saloon keeper's private stock for the better part of an evening.

Dixon savored fine long guns and first-rate whiskey.

Most of his cohorts found his personal aloofness and his preoccupation with firearms somewhat disquieting. With rare exception, most men simply kept their distance. Dixon had few friends, and that number might have exceeded his actual need. .

Everyone now called him merely by his last name, Dixon. On his first buffalo hunt, it was to distinguish him from his age peer and another first-timer, Billy Masterson. To call both Billy was awkward and inefficient, and the affable Masterson seemed to be a "Billy". By the end of the hunt, the name Dixon provided an intimate distance that seemed fitting for the man. So, just Dixon it was.

It was as the buffalo trailed further south that he discovered it was the personality of the land that intrigued him. His passion for roaming this land had overwhelmed his lukewarm desire to kill buffalo.

Dixon not only knew this land, deep in his soul he felt a reverence and devotion to this most inhospitable of places. This vast, flat grassy expanse of prairie confirmed his perception of life's cycles, yet it continually astonished him. Ultimately, it would renew him.

On the Llano Estacado, where others heard nothing and saw little more than nothing, Dixon was coming to see everything. He was coming to know its moods, to understand its sounds and the feel of its air. He knew what belonged and what had resulted from an intruder. Accepting that he himself was an intruder, he was always cognizant that his passing would leave its sign upon the plains. He labored arduously, attempting to leave behind no trace he had passed, but more often than not he learned more about reading the sign of own passing. He had decided that even the bobwhite in the Canadian River bottoms left their marks. He just had not yet learned to fully recognize them.

He loved the simplest and most restrained sounds of the plains. Like the most subtle of variance in musical tones, he heard and appreciated the almost inaudible sounds made by the crackling of dry grass breaking under the buckskin's hooves.

With little question, by 1874, no white man had a more intimate relationship with the southern plains. The Llano Estacado had acquired in Billy Dixon a willing and devoted disciple.

Thirteen

J ust north of the Palo Duro Canyon on the Prairie Dog fork of the Canadian River, Dixon crossed several trails he read as being Comanche and Kiowa having passed the previous day. Within the hour, he cut what he made to be a Comanche track only a few hours old.

He estimated 14 horses, 10 carrying a man's weight, headed southwest on the fast time. Dixon turned, following the sign north and reached a point where he concluded 4 or 5 other Comanche had split from the group, quickly picking up a fast pace to the west.

Dixon continued to follow the fresh track north. Less than an hour on the track, he sighted the crows circling. Too many birds for his liking. He stayed with the sign for another mile or so and then broke track to the east, keeping the breeze in a place he could approach the site from downwind.

As he topped a small knoll, he spotted a pair of wagons on the edge of a grove of cedars. The stench of death was riding on the breeze. He dismounted and rubbed the muzzle of the buckskin. While buffalo camps had conditioned the buckskin to death's smell, on this day Dixon would take no chances. He eased up onto what passed for higher ground on the Llano, keeping the rise between him and the wagons, so he had an unobstructed view of the scene while allowing him to show little of himself.

Dixon could see three bodies. From first glance, Dixon knew the wagons adorned with rattlesnake skins and rattles belonged to Whistlin' Charley. Whistlin' Charley, no last name Dixon knew, he figured Charley had a last name but such things didn't matter much to Dixon. Whistlin' Charley was plenty of names for any one man.

Dixon waited and watched, carefully but quickly assessing the sight below him. He saw no movement beyond the birds.

Dixon now made a more paced assessment of the scene. Charley's two skinners appeared to have been the more fortunate ones, both shot making a run for whatever weapons or cover the wagons might have afforded.

Whistlin' Charley appeared to have not experienced the relative good fortunate of his hired skinners. The Comanche had tied him to a wagon wheel and gutted him while he was alive, spreading his intestines on the ground around him. Then he was left to watch as whatever scavengers found him first and feasted on him.

Dixon didn't care much for Charley when he was alive, viewing him as a wasteful hunter, somehow disrespectful to the animals he killed. Still and all, Dixon wished no man Charley's death.

Dixon removed his binoculars, a gift from an old Priest who had visited him at Fort Sumner, from their case in his possibles bag and took a seat in tall grass. He placed his hat, a Stetson on which he had kept the brim flat and the crown rounded, upon his knee and wiped his forehead with the sleeve of his shirt.

He carefully surveyed the ground below him, confirming the three men were long dead. The hostiles had taken the hands and the ears of the skinners, and a blood stain at the crotch of one of the skinner's pants said that his genitals had been sliced off before death could save him from the situation.

Dixon liked the binoculars, stronger than the 5X Government issue glasses that most officers had. He could come upon a place, view it carefully from a reasonable distance and then leave it undisturbed, showing no sign of his presence or his passing.

He gazed at his hat. It had been a luxuriant pearl gray when he bought it Wichita. Now seasons of West Texas dust and the ruddier sands of New Mexico had been set in the fabric by seasons of scorching sun and monsoon rains, and the hat itself had taken on the color of the landscapes. A pueblo woman outside Fort Sumner had made a hat band of turquoise beads and rawhide with a chin strap that allowed him to secure the hat on even the windiest days.

Beyond even his rifles, Dixon admired his hat.

His focus drifted back to the dead men. It looked to Dixon as if the Comanche had corralled Charley before he could get to his bite, the cyanide-filled Sharps cartridge that most carried in the event such misfortunate should overtake them.

A random thought drifted through his mind. Maybe a curious rattlesnake had taken a good strike and shortened Charley's dying. Charley liked everything about rattlesnakes. Beyond their skin and their rattles, he considered their meat to be the true culinary delicacy of the plains. Dixon liked the idea, the symmetry of a rattlesnake bite sending Charley to dust before he could bleed out. While Charley would not have been big on the idea of his own dying, Dixon thought given the circumstances Charley would have chosen a fine rattlesnake strike as the preferred scheme to send him on his final journey.

Either way, Charley was dead and Dixon was grateful that he didn't have to decide if he wanted to descend through the grass to deliver some final fatal, but merciful stroke.

To bury the men was nothing Dixon gave even a passing consideration. Not that Dixon was concerned that the Comanche party might come back, he just saw no need. Charley was dead and half-eaten anyway. The Llano was a hard place for the birds, and the coyotes too. For anything that lived here. And everything had to eat.

Dixon rose and led the buckskin to the rise, mounted and left.

Throughout the rest of the day Dixon saw enough sign to confirm the plains were unusually active. Active enough to further extend his finely tuned survival sensors.

It was yet another fresh trail and a tight column of smoke moving skyward from near the bottoms of the Salt Fork of the Red that finally presented him with adequate concern, and he decided it was time for him to pay Jim Hanrahan a visit.

Fourteen

*A*t the crack of March of 1874, Dixon had guided a group of Dodge City merchants headed by Charles Rath and Jim Hanrahan, interested in establishing a trading site that would be more convenient for the hunters who were now following the buffalo into West Texas. A trading site close enough that they could drop in for bullets, food, whiskey and a respite from their work, and ultimately quite profitable for the investors.

Dixon guided them to the ruins of an abandoned Bent Brothers fort, a place that had flourished long enough in the 1830's for the Bents to have constructed some substantial adobe buildings.

Dixon stumbled upon the remains during one of his wandering explorations and had taken shelter on a very windy night behind the adobe walls. Come morning, he found himself quite impressed by the seeming sturdiness of the remaining adobe structures, and by their location near the confluence of the Canadian River and a feeder creek. He rested the buckskin for a couple of days near the ample grass and water. Dixon simply enjoyed the sounds and sights of the location.

When approached by Jim Hanrahan, the walls of the abandoned Bent Brothers fort seemed to Dixon to be ideal for the proposed business enterprise.

After he led them from Dodge City to the site, he hadn't lingered. He took half his guide's fee in the form of a new Henry repeating rifle, ample ammunition for the rifle and for his Sharps, along with an agreement concerning Hanrahan's inventory of a particular Kansas City whiskey. The balance he took in gold coin. He expressed his curiosity about the plains to the east of the Palo Duro and the forks of the Red and the Canadian rivers, and he left.

He knew Hanrahan and Rath were industrious, but the sight that greeted him upon his return surprised him. The post had been resurrected, a straight line of five buildings that appeared to be somewhat attached to each other by their common use of the existing adobe ruins. While the adobe, chinked cottonwood log and sod structures blended reasonably into the landscape, the prairie seemed somehow wounded, an old sore re-opened. But Dixon now found most settlements to be rather out of place on the prairie.

A binocular scan, made for no reason other than he liked looking through the binoculars, showed that sod now supported and leveled the strong skeletal adobe walls. Cottonwood timber beams and sod made for substantial roofs. Dixon liked that Hanrahan had utilized the ruin with highest adobe sides for a corral, whose only cottonwood rail side opened directly onto the street, for the horses and mules. The corral's high and solid sides backing toward the creek made the animals a less inviting target for even the most skilled horse thief.

The hider's wagons and several brush arbor sheds built for storing hides made the settlement appear much larger than it actually was.

The number of horses and mules outside the corral, either grazing toward the creek lined with hackberry, cottonwood and elm or in the corral, suggested that he was not the first to become concerned about the activity on the plains.

As Dixon resettled himself in his saddle, he felt a familiar twinge of hesitancy about towns and that many people. As the discomfort passed, he nudged the buckskin toward the settlement, passing a sign proclaiming the place to be Adobe Walls.

Another sign revealed that Tommy O'Keefe had indeed put in a Blacksmith shop, building a cottonwood plank corral along with a structure utilizing old adobe remnants and newly secured sod to construct something that would pass for a livery stable.

He saw Hanrahan had his saloon and it appeared to be thriving. Charles Rath had another general store, but with a neat and newly painted competitor down the way in Myers and Leonard Store. Wedged between the Hanrahan Saloon and Rath's General Store was a building with chinked cottonwood walls whose sign simply read "Eats".

Dixon reined in front of the livery and removed his tack. Tommy O'Keefe came out the front of the livery. A balding red-faced Irishman with the large upper body developed by the men who plied his trade greeted Dixon with an ear-to-ear Irish smile.

"Tommy O'Keefe here," he said, extending his immense hand. "Mighty fine buckskin you be havin'."

Dixon accepted the handshake and simply said, "Dixon."

The smile faded from greeting to an expression of recognition and respect, adding, "Then 'tis even more pleased I am to make the acquaintance." His words could not have carried more sincerity.

Dixon nodded. "Jim in his place?" he asked, motioning toward the saloon.

"Yes. There he'd be," came the quick response, and then added, "Your buckskin will get nothin' but my finest."

Again, Dixon nodded and begin taking off his saddle roll, removing the Henry repeater from its boot. "Leavin' my tack if it suits you."

"Hell of a corral ya got." Dixon said, noting the corral made of thick sharpened posts buried at their base, side by side creating a solid wall of sharpened stakes between Tommy's livery and smithy and Rath's Store.

Tommy nodded, visibly pleased, and responded, "Be no horse taken from here." Tommy was proud of the protection he had provided for his charges in a land filled with horse-thieves of all complexions.

He pointed with great pride to the log doors of the livery. "'Tis built as of a Scottish Castle me Momma spoke to me of. Twas done with some haste though."

Through the vision of castle exceeded Dixon's capacity for imagination, he again nodded his approval. Dixon liked any man who took such pride in his work.

Jim Hanrahan had turned and walked to the end of the bar to the small sod frame opening for respite and fresh air when he spotted Dixon. If there had been no mistaking the hat, the long gait to his stride and the ease of movement would have clearly identified the man who had guided them to this spot.

He stepped from behind the bar and out the door, meeting Dixon a few paces outside the doorway.

"Well, got yourself lost and Old Buck led you in?" Jim smiled.

"Plenty of Comanch sign out there. I figured ya to be in need," Dixon responded with a nod and the closest resemblance of a smile he could muster.

"Got no less than a dozen or so hunters sleepin' on my floor that tells me that. Course they tucked tail in sooner than you. But three of Bull Wickersham's boys drove in from Camp Sweetwater yesterday. Now them's boys don't scare easy, but after coming on a couple of skinned hiders they stopped in for a bit."

Hanrahan paused and then added, "And they hauled in a friend of yours with 'em, Billy Masterson. Boy got his self a gun reputation now. Done gone and blowed Melvin King, Sergeant U. S. Army and one nasty son of a bitch, clean to hell. A deed worth the doin'. Got a new name he's taken a fancy to – Bat, Bat Masterson." Hanrahan chuckled.

In a more somber tone, Hanrahan continued, "Now, King put a round in the boy before he departed to hell. Boy's got a limp, but he's moving good enough." "Damn, Dixon don't you ever answer or ask?"

Reporting a straightforward statement of fact, Dixon said, "I come on Whislin' Charley and couple of his skinners. Charley got gut spread and his skinners had few of their vitals sliced off. Suspect the Comanch took 'em for scare."

Hanrahan looked toward horizon and simply shook his head, then said, "Heard they got a couple of wagons 'round Chicken Creek, too."

"Looks like you got a saloon goin'. Rath got company quick," Dixon said glancing toward the General Store.

"Kinda. Charles has got himself more of an arsenal than a general store. Gun merchant and hide buyer, that's 'bout as wide an inventory as Charles wants. He's in Dodge right now gatherin' up even more. Jim Langdon is here runnin' it," Hanrahan allowed, then added, "Dixon, you can't believe the ammunition he's got in his place. Myers isn't really here, he's off with Rath. Fred Leonard's runnin' the store and he's good people. And O'Keefe, I'd admit he's a little simple minded but he'll love that horse of yours to death and hell, a smith don't have to be overly bright – don't really matter much to a horse."

"Good smith matters a lot." Dixon said. "Who's makin' eats?"

"Bill Olds and his wife. Nice folks and good eats. Charles recommended 'em. Wife is a friend to his missus. We talked 'em into comin' and glad I did," Jim told him and added as an afterthought, "Rath's got one of them new .44 Sharps. Might wanta take a peek at her."

His interest clearly stimulated, Dixon nodded his appreciation of the information.

"Dixon, glad to see ya. Walk a piece with me." When safely out of anyone's earshot, Jim spoke. "Got nine or so hunters sleepin' on my floor, couple of Bull's boy, these ain't boys that hear the Elephant. Somethin' out there ain't right."

Jim continued, "The rest them that's here is shopkeepers, skinners and the like. Might not be a lot of punkin' in a fight.

Army scouting party came through day before yesterday. Sergeant leadin' didn't know horse shit from buffalo chips, but Amos Chapman was with them. Amos feared something was cookin' around the Comanch fires, mostly Quahadis and Kotsotekas, but he also spotted one small group of Tenawa coming toward the Palo Duro."

Dixon stopped, moved some dust with his boot. Hanrahan stayed put and continued. "Seems some crazed Quahadis Holy Man's stirrin' the buffalo stew. A Holy Man full of spit and smokin' the bud can whip up a hell of a stew."

"Quahadis." Dixon became more thoughtful. He stirred the dust into a neat little pile. "Holy Man can stir, but if it's got Quahadis at its heart, then a man's got to worry with that breed Parker. Only half-Comanch, but that half has a real load of sand to spew outta his craw." He kicked the pile of dust he'd made with the toe of his boot. "Amos have his squaw along?"

"Didn't see Mary," Hanrahan answered.

"'Spect he got her safe at her daddy's camp," Dixon advised, and his tone made it clear that he would have liked it better if Amos' wife had been with him, then added, "Lotta Kiowa sign about."

"Dixon, Comanch don't like Rath much and this trading spot has to be a sore," Jim said. "I think the stew that's brewin' might be thick enough to want to cut this wart off."

"Sure it's been noticed. Comanch not gonna miss those stacks of hides ya 'round – be here to kill buffalo – their buffalo. Be like not notin' a boil on your butt," Dixon responded. He continued, "Got a plan to protect your powder?"

"Some, but didn't build no fort here."

"Army tosses up few tents and calls it a fort. You and Rath build a damn fort and called it a town," Dixon observed, then mused, "'Cept for Tommy. He built hisself a castle."

"Ya' know this land," Jim said, seeking help. "Lotta horse thieves."

"How far to the dead tree?" Dixon asked, pointing to a large dead cottonwood, somehow out of place on the sloping grassy hillside.

"192 paces up, 181 back. I stepped it off. Whitewashed this side."

Dixon nodded. "'Bout 185 paces then."

Hanrahan agreed. "Like the whitewash on it?"

"Good marker."

"Noticed the wagons seem a bit spread, might git'em in some." Since Jim didn't disagree, Dixon continued, "Just intend givin' the Comanch them animals grazin' 'tween here and the water?"

"Not mine to move," was Jim's matter of fact reply. Dixon tightened his lips as if disinterested and shook his head in a manner that indicated his concern.

While he knew Jim Hanrahan had more concerns to speak of, Dixon was done for now. "Where's that fresh minted gun hand?

Jim reached to touch Dixon's shoulder, but Dixon shrugged it away. No offense intended and none taken. Jim said, "I'll show ya. Course, ya could just follow your ears to the sound of cards shuffling."

He paused, smiled and added, "I suspect ya'd be wantin' a small glass from our personal inventory." The thought of the private stock brought a tight-lipped smile to Dixon's face.

As they turned, Hanrahan ask in a more solemn voice, "Think Charley got to his bite?"

"No." There was nothing faint in Dixon's response.

"Dixon, good ya here."

"Good to be here." Dixon stopped walking and turned toward the end of the row of structures. Almost as an afterthought he added, "Them that's got the wagon out a ways might want to bring it in some."

"That's the Scheidler brothers, Shorty and Jake. Ain't likely. Just bull-headed Germans. And they're haulin' some gal toward Fort Dodge, gal's got herself pretty bad diseased. Got the cancer in her chest to boot. 'Spect they stay where they be. Ain't part of us no way."

"Should. Them ox looks strong. Good strong stock," Dixon said. "Still too far out." Then he dropped the matter, but the random wagons were a worry.

As they approached the saloon, Billy Masterson, perhaps over-dressed for Adobe Walls with the bowler hat on his head at ever so slight an angle, strolled into the street. His limp was hardly distinguishable, but he seemed to enjoy carrying the cane. A huge smile covered his face when he realized it was Dixon coming toward the saloon with Hanrahan.

"Jim, let me think – skinny to the bone, dusty dirty hat – seems as I know someone like that," Masterson said as they approached.

"No call to speak ill of my hat," was Dixon's reply. He touched the crown of his hat, fixing it firmly on his head. Smiles came hard for Dixon, but he was indeed pleased to his friend. "Don't 'pear too lame to me."

"Sounds as if you ain't been learnin' words. Suppose I'll have to do the talkin' for both of us." Masterson acknowledged Dixon's greeting. "I'm headed to eat over with the Olds, and God knows you look like you can use a meal."

"Ya talk, I chew," came the retort.

"The beef steak'll take some chewing, but it's tasty enough to be worth the effort," Masterson allowed.

"Oh, you know Charles Rath. Nothing but the best for shootin' and eatin'. And he's done plenty of both. Don't expect

Rath will be here often. Lucky to have Jim Langton runnin' the place for him," Masterson said, then added, "Ya got to see the rifles he's got in his place, Sharps to that new Henry, and powder."

Fifteen

*H*annah Olds was an especially attractive woman by frontier standards. She was of such slight build that she had long carried the nickname "Willow", though none called her that to her face. But when it came to the operation of the restaurant, Hannah cooked and kept what her husband called the "cleanest kitchen west of St. Louis".

William Olds had trained as a teacher and was proud of his education, but now he tended to the other tasks of the operation of the restaurant. He cheerfully took the orders, collected the cash and chatted with the clientele. Most in camp noted the kindness with which he treated Hannah. He adored her.

Hannah and William had eloped just after her fourteenth birthday, and they headed west to find a dream.

Most of the men at Adobe Walls envied William Olds, not for his business ties with the rich and powerful Charles Rath, but because he slept with Hannah Olds every night. For most it suggested more than companionship, but also a reliable source of intimate physical contact, something certainly lacking in Adobe Walls as the line at every hog wagon that passed through would attest.

But like many things, it was only an illusion.

While Hannah met what she defined as her marital responsibility, having been unable to conceive a child despite concerted efforts during their early marriage, she considered herself to be a failure in this most feminine aspect of her life. She would tell William, "I'm just dried up."

Most often, after accepting one of her efforts to fulfill her marital obligation, William would agree with her. It was as if his faithful efforts let her know how much she pleased him simply heightened her belief that she was a disappointment. It puzzled her that William continued to be enamored with her, that he enjoyed their talks and was so accepting of what intimacy she felt compelled to provide.

Life in frontier towns often made the women who worked in the saloons and dined in her cafes the only available female conversation. While most often the talk centered about traditional interests, about wishes to be free of the life in which they confessed to find themselves confined, just in conversation they gave Hannah a tip or two on the nature of male sexuality as they had come to understand it, on the efficient pleasing of males. And William did find these most satisfying. She was grateful that he never inquired as to where she learned them.

The occasional restless moment aside, Hannah remained content with her decision to marry William.

While only 31 years old, the frontier had already begun to collect its toll from her. In the late evenings as she prepared for bed, she would use a variety of lotions and patent medicines on her skin. She felt her skin was losing its softness, giving way to a dry and cracking sensation that while unnoticed by others, distracted her. Nonetheless, each evening she carefully dabbed the potions on her skin before going to bed, checking her face each morning in her hand mirror for visible changes.

She would privately try small amounts of some recommended remedies on her more personal areas, hoping to secure a cure to her infertility. The process of applying the remedy would on occasion bring a sensation of pleasant warmth to her personal life that pleased her, giving her hope. Though discovery would have brought her significant embarrassment, it was at these times she would lift her gown and use her hand mirror to check for changes that might somehow suggest an increased possibility of fertility. Hannah desperately wanted children.

Most evenings, after dinner, they sat in the rocking chairs that William had tied to the wagon and brought from Dodge City as they came to Adobe Walls. He had constructed what passed for a porch in Adobe Walls, a place for him to sit and rock with Hannah and talk of their day. There they would rock until Hannah would excuse herself to prepare for bed. It was those rare evenings that Hannah would tell him tell not to tarry long tonight that signaled the most exciting nights of William Olds' married life.

The Olds seemed to simply rock their way through life. Their three months in Adobe Walls were little different than their days in any of the other frontier towns they had lived. So as with their rocking chairs, their lives went back and forth, seemingly moving, yet at the end of the day they found they had gone nowhere.

Sixteen

*H*ats in hands as they entered Eats, Dixon observed, "Be damned – round tables."

Both placed their hats on the chair backs and took a seat.

"Ya know Mr. Rath. He don't come often, but he'll have real tables to eat at when he does," Masterson offered in explanation, "The plates and cups may be as tin as on the trail, but wait 'till you bite into what Mrs. Olds puts in'em. Do you think Mr. Rath is really rich?"

"Rumored out at Sumner that he had two ricks of hides up in Santa Fe last season," Dixon answered.

"80,000 hides brings a lotta cash," Masterson observed.

"Lotta dead buffalo." Dixon's response offered a more sober tone.

William Olds came to the table. "Hello, Bat. Looks as if you've brought a new face with you."

The introductions were brief but to the point.

"It's meatloaf with potatoes today. I think Hannah outdid herself on the meatloaf."

Hannah came from the kitchen with a tin cup in hand. She said, "Mr. Hanrahan said this was three fingers of what you'd be likin'."

"Kind of ya, Ma'am," Dixon said while taking full note of this lovely woman. She silently took note of Dixon's unspoken compliment. There was some pleasure in being noted by such a boy.

"Meatloaf for me." Bat placed his order.

"If not a trouble, I'd like two eggs and beefsteak, not over panned, and potatoes," Dixon requested.

"No trouble, just take a few minutes," Olds said, and then asked already knowing the answer, "Two coffees? New." Bat nodded and Olds left.

"Bat, Bat – do you like bein' called by that?" Dixon asked.

"It sounds right enough," Bat responded.

"If ya get shot all to hell to get it, it ought to," Dixon allowed.

"Hell, Dixon, some of them stories is making me out to be a big hero, shootin' defendin' a woman's honor," Bat said, spreading his arms to emphasize the big concept.

"Who'd be spreadin' such a tall tale?" Dixon asked as he sipped at Hanrahan's private stock.

After an exaggeratedly thoughtful look, Bat said, "Me. At least that's kinda of how I told it to that Austin newspaper fella."

Dixon's chuckle was actually audible. "Shoulda knowed."

"If they're goin' tell whoppers 'bout it, might as well be my whoppers," Bat said, rationalizing his choice.

Dixon shrugged his agreement as he again savored the taste of Hanrahan's best. While Dixon had become a fan of high quality whiskey, he was a bigger fan of keeping his wits about him at all times. The three fingers would last an evening.

The food came and Dixon said, "Tell me the true of it while I eat," knowing full well that his friend would continue with the story of Sweetwater regardless. Bat would talk, pausing on occasion for a bit. Dixon ate good food as he drank good whiskey, slowly but seriously. Finished, he sat back, enjoying the comfort of a chair, the lingering flavor of a beefsteak with a savored sip of the personal select, and soaked in the pleasure of Bat's stories.

"So, you like Bat?" he asked again.

"Has more meat on its bones than Billy, don't ya think?" Billy answered with a question, and then added, "Ya want to go back to being Billy?"

The question gave Dixon a brief pause. Subsequently he said, "Guess people call ya by what makes them easy. Few call Mister Rath anything 'cept Mister Rath."

"Too powerful a fella to call nothing else. Or maybe like callin' you Dixon, respect the both of ya but don't know their ground with either of ya." Bat almost regretted the words as they left his mouth.

Dixon thoughtfully nodded. He seemed to understand without even considering taking offense to Bat's reference to his preference for social isolation.

"Comanch sign bring you in?" Bat asked, seeking a change in topic.

"Some." He nodded. "Some. Lotta sign and not followin' buffalo, no sign of squaws or young'uns . Bothersome sign."

Outside, the friends settled themselves into a seat on a bench in front of Rath's store.

"Damn, it ain't right what they did to Charley and to his boys, cuttin'em down here," Bat said, patting his crotch. "Ain't right." He shook his shoulders and pinched his lips to accent his words. Something of a shudder.

"Comanch figured they own the buffalo, kinda like ranchers and cattle. I spent a couple of weeks with a rancher, Mr. Goodnight, last trip south of the Palo Duro. I'll tell now if you had a rick of his hides in Santa Fe and left the carcasses stinking up his place – well, I just figger he'd be jinglin' your nuts in his pocket right about now."

"Damn, Dixon ya done spent too long with no company, too much time on the lonesome." He paused, then added, "Dixon, ya don't know shit." Then Bat got quiet.

Gesturing, Dixon said, "Moon rise over O'Keefe's. Purty."

Both got quiet.

Dixon sipped the last of the whiskey and got up. He watched his friend use the cane, attempting to raise himself from his seat on the ground, shook his head and said, "Shot up over a whore."

Bat's response was quick. "Damn you, Dixon, I loved Molly."

"Ya don't gotta poke everything ya love." Dixon paused, then added, "Memory serves, ya don't love everything you poke either."

Dixon shook his head again, "Lovin' the whore don't get ya no less shot up."

"Damn you!" Bat blurted, then again thought he needed to learn more words to expresses his aggravation. And even the thought of being outtalked by Dixon greatly exasperated him.

Dixon shrugged.

Bat now fully upright, the pair stepped around the corner and began to walk toward Hanrahan's door.

As the noise from Hanrahan's reached his ear, Dixon hesitated and then came to a full stop. Masterson, now a couple of paces ahead, turned to look back at him.

"Billy, go ahead. Think I'll rest a bit over behind Eats. Looked nice," Dixon said as he retreated from the noise, from the confinement waiting inside the saloon.

Masterson replied, "Think I'll play a hand or two before I call it a night."

Dixon nodded, although Masterson was already walking toward Hanrahan's, then added, "Tell Jim I'll be behind Eats."

With that Dixon turned away from the sights and sounds of Hanrahan's Saloon and went to O'Keefe's to pick up his blanket roll. He made his way toward the now darkened Eats.

The Olds' porch afforded the only potential exposure to the open plains in the otherwise solid exterior of the buildings of Adobe Walls, a fact that had not escaped Dixon's note.

Although unintended, the silence of his approach startled the Olds, who were rocking on their porch.

They acknowledged each other and Dixon advised, "Goin' to take my rest near the cottonwoods. I'll bother ya none."

Away from the sounds of Hanrahan's, Dixon was soon resting in a spot that gave him a clear line of sight out onto the plains. He could see the back of Eats and of Charles Rath's armory disguised as a store.

The breeze softened and moon was almost full. Sleep came comfortably.

Part Three

Palo Duro Canyon
June 1874

Seventeen

A mbiguity frustrated Quanah, although the totality of his life was defined by its ambiguity. It was an underlying sense of the inevitable that most often guided him. He trusted the council of no man's logic above the conclusions of his own intellect. Yet the quite logical and fatalistic 24 year-old Quanah found comfort and placed confidence in the wisdom the peyote pipe revealed, a spiritual experience he judged to expand his mind, allowing the consideration of prospects he may have otherwise rejected.

He made his way up to a favored outcropping that gave him a view westward up the canyon, and ultimately of the sunset. From this vantage point as the half-light of evening begin to settle upon the canyon, he would view the camp below him settling in for the night. He found reason and comfort in the canyon and in the camp.

The canyon was governed by the unyielding laws of nature to which it must comply. The campsite reflected the fierce individuality and the autonomy so coveted by every Comanche. Yet the women in their orderly settling of the camp for nightfall brought a solid predictability to the coming darkness, a well choreographed ballet of life performed nightly upon the canyon floor.

The Palo Duro Canyon had been carved into the plateaus of the high southern plains by the Prairie Dog Town Fork of the Red River over a million years ago. Quanah found a reverence in the solitude and beauty of this vista the Great Spirits had provided for the Quahadis.

Quanah approached both religion and holy men with considerable caution, both at times angering him as they used the spiritual nature of the people to gain status or control, contrary to the highly sovereign principle entrenched in the culture and character of the Nermernuh, the People. Such reservations, however, did not impair his ability to view this wonder of creation as quite spiritual. It was here in the canyon he could reach out to his father for wisdom, courage and guidance.

The canyon was spiritual and mystical, concealing in its walls the very secrets of life itself. Quanah was convinced all of his Nermernuh ancestors had preceded him into the canyon and left all of their knowledge contained in its walls, to be revealed to the deserving seeker.

The Palo Duro Canyon had provided shelter and food for the nomadic peoples who inhabited the region as far back as oral tradition could carry such memories. The length and width of the canyon provided safety from intruders and gave shelter from the wildly erratic weather of the Great Plains. Its mesquite and juniper provided an abundant supply of high quality hardwood for needs ranging from lodge poles to fragrant cooking fires to weapons for the hunt. Its streams afforded clear clean water, and the murky waters of the Red River provided a generous supply of water in the dry seasons, allowing for grassy meadows on which the treasured Comanche horses could graze. Except for the crucial buffalo, the Palo Duro provided an idyllic environment for the Comanche of the last half of the nineteenth century.

Quanah loved his world and his life.

While it was Quanah's view that no man could actually own the land upon which they stood, he did believe the Quahadis were the primary custodians of this wonder of nature.

As with the children now playing below him, it had been his playground as a child. Although his mother, Sally Ann Parker, was a white captive, the influence of his father, Peta Nocona, brought him equal status with the other boys. His skills and daring separated him from them. And he remembered the great infatuation his father and his mother seemed to have with each other.

Quanah had warm memories of his childhood in this natural playground. Then in early adolescence, upon his return from the white world, the canyon was the pathway to his spiritual world. The canyon was predictable. The canyon was reliable.

It was his wonderings in the canyon that gave stability to his life as he struggled to reassert his position among his Quahadis peers and to define his emerging manhood upon his return from the white man's Texas.

He had been taken to the white world by the Texas Rangers who "rescued" his mother in 1860 when Quanah was 10, returning her to a life from which she had been absent for 24 years, to a life she could never again embrace.

While her three children were with her, it was her daily expectation that her husband would again ride in and take her captive. She longed for his company and the life they shared. But she would realize her husband's now severely arthritic body made simple movements challenging and a heroic rescue impossible. Yet, she dreamed.

The strange odors and the harsh, sharp sound of the voices of the Texas Rangers who rescued his mother along with his baby sister, Prairie Flower, and his infant brother, Pecos, from the tranquil summer hunting camp clung to his mind, at times encroaching into his consciousness in quite negative fashions. He had sensed the Rangers' contempt for him and he reciprocated in kind.

When word reached his mother of her husband's death from an infected wound, the sadness settled deep into her soul, never to leave those depths.

He only recalled his mother as sad after that time. His younger brother, Pecos, contracted the pox and died. Then his adored sister Prairie Flower died of influenza. His mother was overwhelmed by the death of her husband and of her two youngest children. It was as if only death and despair dwelled in this strange world of the white man.

Quanah watched as his Mother starved herself to death. He felt had she been able to find adequate value in him, she might have found the motivation to sustain her desire to live. But he knew that was not his mother's truth. She valued her eldest greatly. Her rare words would voice encouragement for him to return to the world of his father's people. The image of his mother's demise was etched so firmly into his consciousness that he was rarely without it.

He somberly watched as the white men buried his mother next to his siblings. Then, under the blanket of night, he slipped from the confines of Anderson County, Texas, and made his way toward the country of the canyon.

He thought of his mother as he sat on the outcropping overlooking everything that he now held dear in his life. He had come to increasingly understand her sorrows.

Quanah blamed the Texas Rangers for all the ills that befell his family. He loathed the Texas Rangers. He loved his mother and would try to vicariously ease her burden for the rest of his life. There was the pervasive feeling he should not have let the white man bury her at the site of her great misery. Contemplations of this lapse haunted him.

His return to the canyon, to the Nermernuh, was greeted with suspicion. Even the son of Peta Nocona, after almost four years in the white world, must prove himself beyond all doubt. He worked harder at being Quahadis than any other did. He strived to embody every aspect of being Quahadis.

Eighteen

Q uanah lifted himself from his seated position on the outcropping and for a moment gazed out beyond the canyon into a purplish cloud trimmed in orange as the sun still lingered beneath the horizon. He pulled his posture to its most upright position, drew in a deep breath, catching just a whiff of juniper, and released it into a long sigh. Resolution was coming to Quanah. The manifest would come.

He turned to the canyon wall behind him and touched it with both hands fully opened and palms extended in full contact with the stone. He searched for his father, for the guidance of his ancestors. The traces of tension faded and his face relaxed as he increased the pressure of his hands upon the rock.

While the guidance he received most often confirmed the conclusions to which he had already arrived, it nonetheless brought confidence and reassurance. The spiritual guidance given by his ancestors provided an indisputable source of support, enhancing his conviction as to the correctness of his beliefs.

Weakeah, glancing at the outcropping, saw her husband arise, turn and extend his arms toward the canyon wall. The sight of her husband pleased her, as it most often did. He was broad-faced and thick boned, but he stood so erect that his figure silhouetted against the sky in the ever-dimming light of the canyon was unmistakable.

She knew tonight around the council fire there would be judgments made about which her husband would have strong opinions, but he would hold his silence. It was not yet the time to speak of the inevitable outcomes that he foresaw. In talking with her under the robes of morning, he had shared with her his thoughts, his belief that the Nermernuh can only hear such a truth when time has prepared them for such a harsh but foreseeable certainty.

Her husband had held her tightly and spoke softly as he stroked her hair. "You cannot rush the Nermernuh to a hard truth until the dreams of a return of the old ways are gone. As with my mother, given time the white man will overwhelm and kill the dream. But for now they dream and believe in the medicine of Eschiti. I cannot steal that from them."

It was this gentle side of her husband that she adored; she believed it to have come from his white time. The sharing and exchanging of thoughts under the robes during the intimate warming caresses of morning was not the Comanche way she heard from other wives.

Weakeah knew her husband would come soon. She would have food ready even though he would likely eat little, more moving the food from spot to spot in the Mexican bowl while eating an occasional small morsel. He would speak with her, he would be grateful for her efforts but he would be lost in his thoughts.

Quanah made his way back down the slopes to the camp and sat at his wife's cook fire. They spoke little. He touched the back of her hand and allowed his fingers to linger there for a moment when she gave him the Mexican bowl he enjoyed. The rabbit and roots were flavorful, but his thoughts of the coming council preoccupied him.

The camp was settling and the children's play was quieting. He watched as three young boys now tossed pebbles at a larger stone some 10 paces from them. Quanah enjoyed watching the play.

Weakeah knew her husband well and loved him greatly.

He now turned his attention to watching the arrival of others as they came to take their place around the council fire, waiting until most had arrived, especially Eschiti. Quanah wanted to time his arrival so that his appearance would interrupt and abbreviate the accounts of mystical magic that Eschiti would be spinning.

Weakeah stepped behind Quanah and adjusted the set of the single eagle feather in his left braid. Then she quickly moved on, and he rose from the comfort of their fire.

Quanah positioned his buckskin poncho, stretched himself to full height and moved to take his place in the council circle.

Weakeah now sat and watched her husband move away from their fire. Something in his movements led her to recall the first day she believed that he had noticed her. A small group of three young men had gone in search of horses to steal. In celebration, the first two budding warriors rode into camp at full voice, extremely proud of the single horse each had secured. As they settled, Quanah rode slowly and deliberately across the creek with his three horses in tow. He sat his mount straight backed and straight faced until he came before the group of girls in which Weakeah stood. He looked directly at her and smiled. She was completely smitten with the handsome young man, now the proud owner of three new ponies.

Her father, Ekitaocup, was considerably less thrilled about his daughter's infatuation with Quanah. After several months of clandestine courtship filled with secret meetings between the love-struck couple, Quanah approached Ekitaocup concerning marriage. After emphatically denying the couple's request, Ekitaocup repeatedly made slanderous verbal protestations to all who would listen about this son of a white captive.

Weakeah still glowed at the memory of how Quanah had left the village for several days, and upon returning took her from her bed, placed her upon a pony and the young lovers eloped into the prairie. They rode until they reached the western edge of the canyon and a small cave on a rock ledge, a romantic grotto which Quanah had prepared with a buffalo robe, blankets, food and firewood. They honeymooned in a paradise, the 15-year-old Quanah and his bride, who had yet to pay her first visit to the cleansing hut.

After a week, they were joined by four other young men. Over the two years that followed, Quanah led a small but ever growing band on increasingly more successful raids into Texas. His group of followers grew to over a dozen young men, some bringing their budding families with them.

Quanah was gaining status and recognition as a courageous and ferocious warrior. His reputation as a skilled leader was rapidly expanding. He now was a man who commanded respect, an acceptable son-in-law.

After four years, a more accepting Ekitaocup requested that his daughter return and bring her husband with her.

Nineteen

$\mathcal{N}$ ow at 24 years of age, Quanah walked toward his seat at the most significant Nermernuh council to be held in the memory of any of those present. He took his seat next to Howeah, who was among the first to join him and who Quanah considered to the steadiest and trusted the most of those who rode with him. Howeah had never failed to go on an excursion Quanah had undertaken.

Quanah was undecided about the presence of the Kiowa at the council circle. He trusted Lone Wolf to hold his silence and be stubbornly directed by his desire to sustain the existing way of the Kiowa. All the Kiowa would demonstrate the same dogged individuality of the Nermernuh.

While the gathered clans might be the greatest horse cavalry ever assembled, the very thought of acting in unison under the orders of another warrior challenged their most essential instinct of personal autonomy. A Comanche warrior might follow a man he respected into the wildest of prairie fires, but he would never consider surrendering his independence.

His thoughts drifted from the ally to his enemy. While the blue coat soldiers might appear rag-tag at times, Quanah had seen the white man repeatedly fight as a unit. Individually none were the equal of a Comanche warrior on horseback, but as a group following the guidance of an experienced leader, they were formidable. In battle, unity and discipline were the white man's strengths.

For Quanah, the key to victory had always been in the careful and patient selection of the ground upon which to meet his foe. All the camp talk of destroying the encampment at the place of the rotting walls concerned him. He considered waiting for a small group to leave such an encampment, engaging them on the open prairie at a place and hour of his choosing, and there completely destroying his enemy. That constituted the sound policy of triumph.

Quanah found the structured niceties of the beginnings of a council too droll since the death of Buffalo Hump. He missed the oratory of Buffalo Hump, who could make the most formal of opening statements sound important and meaningful and do it with such skill that many did not know if they had just been gravely insulted or highly complimented. Still, Quanah recognized the need for such polite formality. So he settled into his place and the talks began.

After the medicine man, White Wolf, had completed the formal pronouncements, Sun Sound rose to speak. "The white man is again at the mud fort on the Canadian, the place of the rotting walls. The great white hide man is there. The Rath is there. It is a bad thing for both the Kiowa and the Comanche. The Dirty Hat led them there or they would have never found this place, only the Dirty Hat could have found the place of the rotting walls. Now, the Rath builds them new and strong. So strong that even when the cold winds come blowing off the snows of the mountains, the white man will not go back to the Kansas place. The white man can stay at the Canadian forever. I do not think it is a good thing for the Rath, the great collector of hides, to have a place in our lands so that he may send his buffalo killers to slaughter our herds at his whim."

General sounds of accord rose from most at the council circle. Several spoke briefly in agreement.

Then, the young medicine man Eschiti rose. He was an unimposing figure, only barely over 5 feet tall and frail with a thin hawkish face and piercing eyes, but with a voice that sounded as if belonged to Buffalo Hump himself.

He walked slowly around the circle, engaging the eyes of each man assembled as if his glance was somehow penetrating the concealed thoughts of each man, as if he were preparing to expose the thoughts of each man to the entire gathering.

He began. "For four days, I fasted and smoked the magical pipe. I rode the vapors of the smoke into the clouds. There in the mist of the clouds, great wisdom was revealed to me. I, Eschiti, alone was allowed to view the future that might belong to Nermernuh and their Kiowa brothers. The Great Spirits prophesied a return of the buffalo. I, Eschiti, saw enormous herds of buffalo coming to the mouth of the canyon of the Nermernuh, herds so large the ground shook beneath their hoofs. There to save Nermernuh because they were no longer being slaughtered by the white men. The buffalo were grateful to the Nermernuh."

The men gathered at the council listened intently. They had been told by their fathers and their grandfathers of the times in which such herds were abundant from the Nermernuh plains to the land of the Lakota in the north. Just the thought of the return of such herds to the plains brought a muted but audible sigh of approval from the gathering. Desperate men in desperate times responding to the promise of better times.

And these were desperate times in the survival of the Nermernuh. And in the visions of Eschiti, there was hope.

"The Nermernuh and the Kiowa hunting together, sharing in the Great Spirits' reward for driving the white buffalo killers from the land the Great Spirits had given them. The Great Spirits have tricked the Rath. He is at the place of the rotting walls on the Canadian so that we might destroy him and prove ourselves once again worthy of the great reward they had given us, the mighty buffalo. Now, we must reveal our confidence in the guidance of the Great Spirits."

Eschiti reached to the ground, lifted a clay jar and held it above his head. Again he made the slow walk around the circle, his eyes piercing the face of each man. On occasion he stopped in front of a man and with subtle movements of his fingers caused the jar to appear to tremble vigorously, making it appear that the jar's contents were moving it and that he was struggling to contain the power within the jar.

Convinced he had mesmerized his audience, he continued, "Now, the Great Spirits revealed to me there is but this final opportunity to secure the return of the buffalo and rid of lands of the white curse."

He closed his eyes, tilted his head skyward and extended his arms, holding the jar up as if displaying it for the Great Spirits to see. Then, with his voice at its most commanding pitch, he spewed, "This way has been revealed to Eschiti. The way has been shown to Eschiti!"

Lowering the jar and clutching it to his heart, he settled his voice and again slowly walked around the council circle. Eschiti said, "In this jar is a potion made from the walls of the canyon and the remains of the buffalo. In this potion is the magic that will prevent the bullets of the white man from penetrating the skin of a warrior who truly believes."

"Nermernuh shall fall upon the buffalo killers at the daybreak and smother them in a great morning wind of death. The buffalo killers will never awaken from their sleep."

"The Great Spirits have promised no warrior will be without bullets. The Great Spirits have pledged when the cartridges are spent, I, Eschiti will be empowered to belch cartridges from my bowels. The Great Spirits have promised the buffalo to those who follow the path that has been revealed to Eschiti. The Great Spirits say we are to attack the rotting walls and destroy the mighty Rath. These things we must do."

He paused, took an exaggerated deep breath and appeared to allow his eyes to follow the smoke of the council fire skyward, then concluded, "All is there for those who believe the revelations of the Great Spirits as given to Eschiti." Appearing to be exhausted, Eschiti sat.

Quanah gazed directly into the fire. He thought dirt and buffalo dung will protect the true believer, so says Eschiti the self-proclaimed prophet. Quanah understood Eschiti would simply proclaim any wounded warrior not to be a true believer. Eschiti spoke the religion of self-promotion. Quanah remained the skeptic.

But he recognized he was surrounded by many true believers, or at least men who needed urgently to believe that there was a way to stem the tide of the white plague that was devouring their lands, consuming their way of life.

The ordinarily stoic Lone Wolf got his feet to speak. Lone Wolf's rising caught Quanah's attention, bring him back from his own thoughts to the discussion. He brushed an annoying pebble from beneath his rump as he resettled. Any words by Lone Wolf merited his full consideration.

Lone Wolf was uncomfortable even speaking before a small gathering of Kiowa, much less such a group as now sat in the council circle. But he stood, paused to gather himself for the words he wanted to speak.

"I do not speak to judge the wisdom or the medicine of Eschiti. I speak only of what Lone Wolf knows."

"As a very young man, I sat on a rise with many of our brothers near the healing lodge where the Medicine meets the Elm. I heard the white leaders speak of their need for our land. I know now they came to speak false words beside our sacred medicine lodge. I know now it was when Satanta spoke for us, for all the Kiowa, that I heard the truth. Satanta said all the land south of the Arkansas belongs to the Kiowa and the Comanche, and that we should give away none of it.

"He told the white men he did not want a reservation for the children of the Kiowa, that he wanted the children raised as he was raised. As I was raised and as each of us gathered in this circle were raised. He said if he were not free to roam the plains that he would grow pale and die. He spoke the truth for us all.

"I, Lone Wolf, say this land is ours, but now, again the white man cuts down our trees and kills our buffalo. I, Lone Wolf, heard a blue coat soldier standing near the medicine lodge say the Great Sheridan sent by the Great White Leader said if you kill all the buffalo and you will kill all the Kiowa – all the Comanche. The buffalo killers mean to destroy us one buffalo at a time, unless we destroy the buffalo killers.

"The white leaders agreed the land between from the Arkansas to the Red was not to be theirs, but even now the white buffalo killers are at the mud fort on the Canadian. They come to kill the buffalo. When there are no more buffalo there will be no more Kiowa – no more Comanche.

"From the Arkansas to the Red, this land is ours. We do not need the blessing of the white man to say what is ours is ours. The land is ours.

"If we do not place fear in the hearts of the buffalo killers, our children will come to live in white man's houses, the hearts of our children will grow pale and they will no longer be Kiowa – or be Comanche. And we will have let this thing happen to them.

"I do not know of the visions of Eschiti, nor of his medicine, but I know the truth of the white men who would destroy us.

"I, Lone Wolf, and all the Kiowa who choose to join me will ride beside those who will place fear in the hearts of the buffalo killers. It is as Satanta spoke at the Medicine Lodge, all the land from the Arkansas to the Red must be ours, now and for our children's children."

He looked toward Quanah and Howeah and said, "Every white man wants the Kiowa and the Comanche gone from this land. If we keep our rifles silent, we will watch this happen."

Lone Wolf knew the words were now leaving him, he knew he'd spoken his heart. He had spoken enough. He sat and said no more.

Quanah looked across the circle at Lone Wolf and nodded his agreement. Lone Wolf's thoughts were deep and his anger was great.

Several others in the circle now spoke, endorsing and witnessing their belief in the medicine that the Great Spirits had delivered to them through Eschiti.

Convinced that all had spoken, Quanah rose. He began to walk slowly around the circle, but in the opposite direction that Eschiti had walked and closer to the center of the circle, nearer the fire. The embers and glowing light of the fire produced a dynamic framing that changed with each step he took and at times made the single large eagle feather in his braid appear to be floating about his head. Quanah would not speak of mystical experiences, but his appearance provided those at the council with the illusion that it was an extraordinary man who appeared before them.

"I, Quanah, cannot measure the strength of the medicine Eschiti brings to us." Had Quanah spoken otherwise, many at the circle would know he had not spoken the truth.

He continued, "I have proven many times that I do not need the courage of the medicine to do battle with the enemies of the Quahadis. I will not let our enemies believe I need medicine to defeat them. I, Quanah, will fight the enemies of the Quahadis. If in battle, the Great Spirits choose to take me from these plains, then such is their choice. I will enter battle without fear and as I am, a Quahadis warrior. But I speak only for myself, I speak for Quanah."

Without stopping his slow paced walk, he lapsed into a thoughtful silence before continuing. "I believe in the visions of the peyote smoke. I favor any man following any medicine that will bring defeat to the white man, the buffalo killers or to those who would build their houses by our streams and claim our land to be their own." Quanah opened the door to more than just a battle at the place of the rotting walls.

"I do battle with all who wrong Nermernuh. I, Quanah, have a quarrel with any man who brings harm to the Quahadis."

Quanah sat, but the broad nature of his concluding statements was not lost on many at the council. Eschiti knew while Quanah might be a fierce warrior in this cause, he was not a true believer.

Quanah and Lone Wolf held their peace as the gathering decided that the medicine and the visions of Eschiti would provide the guidance for an attack upon the buffalo killers at the rotting walls, that the Rath must be killed. Both knew that ultimately every warrior would fight in the manner of their choosing.

The gravity of the decision of the council seemed to weigh upon most of its participants. They chose to forego the social interchange that often followed the conclusions of these gatherings. Mostly somber men made their own paths away from the council fire. Quanah and Howeah had stepped away together.

Judging them to be beyond earshot of the others, Quanah inquired of Howeah, "You spoke with Quiet Pony?"

Howeah nodded he had and said, "Quiet Pony watched the men at the rotting walls for five days and was never noticed. He saw the Rath's store, but not the Rath. He saw hide wagons come into the place of the rotting walls while he watched, he judged about twelve buffalo killers to be there now with the store men. And already many hide stacks."

"But he did not see the Rath himself?"

"No Rath. He said on his way back he saw Dirty Hat riding in the direction of the rotting walls, but he seemed in no hurry."

"Dirty Hat is never in a hurry," Quanah responded. "Dirty Hat respects the land." Quanah thought and then spoke, "If more whites were like Dirty Hat, there would be no need for this fight."

"Dirty Hat led the Rath to the place of the rotting walls," Howeah snapped.

Quanah nodded in acknowledgment of the latter fact, not wishing to be disagreeable about a dilemma that had no reasonable resolution. He then asked, "What else came to Quiet Pony's eyes?"

"He said the Rath has made the walls stronger and covered the tops with our prairie, that the buffalo killers could have much food and water in their stores. No wall opens to the prairie except one side, and the openings are all small. He says there is only one way in and one way out of the place of the rotting walls, but I think about that he is wrong."

Again, Quanah was thoughtful. "Quiet Pony has done well by us. Tell him so. Has he told anyone else of what he saw?"

"No, and he says he will tell what he saw to no one else."

An image of the place of the rotting walls closed to the prairie on two sides came to him, like heading ponies into a box arm of the Palo Duro. It was disquieting. Quanah liked to attack the white man as he hunted the buffalo, on the open prairie, and to separate them one at a time from the herd, then make the kill. The Quahadis on horseback had no equal. This would not be the way at the rotting walls.

He grasped Howeah by the shoulder and then moved away toward where Weakeah would be waiting. After a few paces, he stopped and turned, looking up at the outcropping from which he had descended in the darkness of the early evening. A vision of the buffalo killers with their many long guns came to him. He did not like the place of the rotting walls.

Twenty

Q uanah sat with Weakeah. He sipped the cool water she had
collected for them from the clay jug. As few of those from
the council would have done, he spoke with her of the place of
the rotting walls. She gave him insights from the other wives.

"Do you hear of the Kiowa, Lone Wolf? He spoke well of
what he knew and I think he will fight well. Do you hear of
him?" Quanah inquired.

"He brought no woman with him. Wolf Run has many wives
and invited him to visit with Jumping Rabbit as he desired. He
has only visited her once. His pain is so deep, he was harsh with
her. He hurt her a little as he visited her. She says he never spoke
a single word." Weakeah always looked toward her feet as she
spoke of such things.

"What do you think?"

"I think I am glad that I eloped with a boy with few ponies."
She smiled and reached out to pat his inner thigh. Quanah smiled.

Then Quanah, again somber, said, "The fight at the place of
the rotting walls will be for warriors. I trust Lone Wolf to fight
well at the place of the rotting walls. Lone Wolf is a warrior."

Quanah sipped the last of his water. He too was thankful that
Weakeah had chosen to elope with a boy who had but a few
ponies.

As camp outside quieted and the night deepened, Weakeah
moved close to her husband. She let her fingers softly drift across
his upper body. As she sensed his breathing quicken she laid her
palm flat upon his chest. Lying on her side, she moved so that he
could not fail to notice the feel of her naked body. She tilted her
head ever so slightly, bringing her lips close to his neck, and she
spoke to him with a breathy whisper. That she aroused him still
delighted her.

After a time as she became more acutely aware of her own
special heaviness, she moved above him, found him and then she
ever so gently eased herself upon him. His hands reached up to

hold and caress her. Soon she once again knew the singularly unique place she held at the very core of his being.

Weakeah dozed beside him and listened to the sounds of his breathing in a deep and tranquil sleep. It was an accepting peace. A place to which she had first accompanied him long ago, a place of tranquility to which on this night she had guided them once again.

Soon enough there would battles to be fought, but not tonight. Tonight Quanah and Weakeah existed in a tranquil world created by their unwavering attachment to each other.

Quanah awakened just as the night was beginning to lift. Weakeah was lying as close to him as he remembered when sleep had taken him. His hand stroked her hair and he moved even closer to her. She had already roused from her sleep, but was basking under the robes on the cool spring morning. She threw both arms around him, quickly springing from under the robes, then draping her doeskin dress over her body in seemingly one fluid movement.

She smoothed out the dress, secretly pleased that her shape had not rounded. She would have traded this sprightly body to have given Quanah a son. But it had just not yet come to pass. Quanah followed her and sat by the cooking fire, enjoying her movements as she began the bustle of the morning.

When she was close, he brushed her cheek and allowed his eyes to linger upon her neck. As he did, he took a breath capturing the air deep in his lungs and slowly released it toward the canyon. It was a sigh that blended appreciation, anticipation and resignation, the creation of acceptance.

He finally spoke. "I am going deep into the canyon for a few days. Here in the camp, there will be at least two days of prayer and preparation. This will be the time in which Eschiti will spread his medicine. I cannot be in the camp when Eschiti places his medicine on the warriors who desire it. While I don't desire his medicine, it is best not to publicly refuse it. I will not be his excuse when the rotting walls become more difficult than he has promised the council. There can be no reason to blame Quanah for bad medicine."

Weakeah asked, "The rotting walls could be a bad place for the Quahadis?"

Quanah nodded yes and expanded. "For all Nermernuh, but I will try not let it become so. But first, I will seek the wisdom of the canyon."

Shortly, he sought out Howeah. Quanah said, "It is my intent to be away when Eschiti begins spread his potion."

Howeah hesitated. "You are not going to partake of what might be such powerful medicine?"

Quanah detected a crack in his ally. "Do you want Eschiti's medicine, my friend?"

Howeah responded, "It might possess the magic that he says."

"But Eschiti said you must be a true believer. Howeah, my friend, are you a true believer?"

"When the bullets of buffalo killers start to come, I might become one."

"Then you should receive Eschiti's medicine, my friend." The words of his friend affirmed what Quanah had suspected. His decision to visit the canyon was a wise judgment.

Quanah left and Eschiti spoke the promises of the Great Spirits and painted the true believers with his potion of protection. No less than fully committed warrior could come to Quanah and ask his beliefs.

Quanah returned from the canyon at sunrise on the third day. The Kiowa had already left for the place of the rotting walls, not wishing to insult the medicine of their allies, but it was not Kiowa medicine.

Eschiti had placed the potion on the chest of each of the warriors of Nermernuh, but only after asking them if they truly believed in the power of his potion.

Weakeah sat beside Quanah as he cleaned and polished his Henry repeating rifle and counted his cartridges. She had prepared him a buckskin food bag with the nature of the journey in mind, and filled two bladders with water. If she had fear, she did not show it. Weakeah was the wife of Quanah and she would carry herself thusly.

The Nermernuh warriors, filled with a sense of invincibility, departed to destroy the Rath and the buffalo killers gathered at the rotting walls.

Twenty-One

*A*s June was fading, with the sun setting behind them obstructing the vision of any of the buffalo killers gathered below him who might take a glimpse toward the grassy mound, Quanah, Howeah and Lone Wolf lay peering at the line of mud buildings all single file with wagons irregularly parked around them.

Wagons could be quickly set afire, but the mud walls were visibly another matter. The place of the rotting walls was no longer rotting.

Quanah shared thoughts. "Eschiti's prophecy foretells the buffalo killers dying before they wake in the morning. I hope his prophecy saw all of them sleeping in their wagons."

"They like to sleep near their wagons," said Lone Wolf, attempting to add an optimistic note to the discussion, "And there are many ponies to be taken."

Quanah agreed. "Great victory might be found in a large number of new ponies."

"We will plunge upon them like the winds of great storm and blow the buffalo killers from our plains. The place of the rotting walls will be no more. Those are words that the Great Spirits have given to Eschiti to speak to the Nermernuh," Howeah asserted.

Quanah was beginning to find his friend irritating. Lone Wolf acted as if he had not heard the words or the slight to the Kiowa. Quanah directed his words to Lone Wolf. "You will get the pony herd by the creek while that first great wind is blowing?" Lone Wolf nodded that he understood how distracted the buffalo killers would be at the onset. Lone Wolf liked the idea of many ponies.

Howeah snorted his disapproval.

"Howeah, my friend, it is like looking at woman. Your heart is deceiving your eyes. The walls of this place are no longer rotting."

"The Rath has made the scar on our land grow larger, another reason he must be blown away by the coming wind," Howeah answered and crawled back below the crest of the knoll, leaving Quanah and Lone Wolf to continue their observation. Howeah saw no point in it. Eschiti had already pointed the path.

Quanah continued, "At least eight wagons are buffalo killers' wagons. They carry men long guns and rifles."

Lone Wolf added, "The three wagons that have camped away from the walls are not buffalo killers."

Quanah nodded his agreement. "I hope that Eschiti has seen clearly and they die before they can wake."

Quanah started to back off the knoll. "Strong walls are troubling. Get the pony herd first."

They left the knoll. Morning would reveal the answers soon enough.

Part Four

Adobe Walls
June 1874

Twenty-Two

*M*en come to measure the success of their lives by quite diverse standards, from their families of origin to their property and possessions. No such vagueness afflicted the Scheidler brothers.

Tight, uncaring, selfish, and German as if the word was an adjective rather than a noun were the expressions others often chose to describe Jacob "Shorty" and Isaac "Ike" Scheidler, two brothers who had immigrated from Germany together some ten years earlier. While the sentiments might have accurately described the observable behavior of the brothers and their lack of participation in traditional frontier social interactions, such descriptions did not depict the true stance of the brothers. By any assessment, they were hard-working and capitalist entrepreneurs. They believed that with hard work and reasonable risk, they could achieve a position of respect in society. They placed great value upon the binding nature of their word, but their trust of others was limited. Trust was generally reserved for immigrants with a European heritage similar to their own.

They foresaw themselves as becoming successful freighters, the primary supplier of goods to the German immigrants whose farms were now beginning to populate the Kansas prairie and the Indian Territory.

To acquire this desired status, they came to assess progress in the acquisition of fine oxen. The value of an ox was measured in durability and strength, stock that could pull the sturdy and extraordinarily well-maintained wagons they were acquiring, a commitment to attaining a strong business and financial foundation while having little interest in the frills of life.

Their fierce independence and unrelenting pursuit of profit made the brothers the focus of resentment from many, and the fruits of their efforts made them the envy of most. Others were suspicious of this conservative approach to the acquisition of business possessions, especially when such prosperity visited few others on the prairie.

The Scheidler brothers accepted no aid for which they did not pay, and they provided no assistance for which they were not paid.

They came to Adobe Walls not because of the activity on the plains, but in the hopes of filling out the third wagon that they had added late with only a partial load when they agreed to escort Nettie Mae, on the condition she drove a team, to Wichita where she could catch the train on to St. Louis for medical treatment. They came by way of Adobe Walls hoping to find Mr. Rath with a surplus of hides in need of delivery.

Given the erratic path of life since her mother gave birth to her in a Kansas City brothel, Nettie Mae had begun to find comfort in the consistent, repetitive lifestyle of the trail with the Scheidler brothers. Despite her initial reservations, she found they made no demands of her beyond those which were agreed upon as payment for her transport to health care. Nothing in Nettie Mae's personal history suggested any man would value her for anything other than her sexuality. So she found the Shadler brothers' general disinterest somewhat confusing, but it was a pleasant and refreshing confusion.

Since the brothers preferred to prepare their own evening meals, she had begun to repair their well-worn clothing, and considering the general state of their garments she found this to be no small undertaking. However, when Ike or Jake expressed their genuine pleasure over a restored garment, it gave her a sense of value that had been so often absent in all other elements of her life.

While driving the wagon or while darning garments, she now allowed thoughts of the past, of her life to enter her conscious awareness. Logic dictated to her that she did have a father, but to the best she could tell Nettie Mae was the only name her mother had given her. She had when occasion required used a last name of convenience, but most often she only went by Nettie Mae.

The trip she was undertaking with Ike and Shorty required no formal name, but the thought of seeking medical treatment for the diseases that now plagued her made her feel compelled to select a more formal, a more complete name. She had no identifiable sense of family, which made finding an acceptable name more challenging than she had anticipated.

She did remember her mother's last name, English, but she had no desire to adopt the name of the woman who had sold her in the brothel to a banker from the St. Joseph area when she was still a girl. A mother who arranged for the abortion that left her barren when she became pregnant at 13, a mother who was angry with her because she could no longer sell her daughter for the virgin premium to customers who were all to willing to be deceived, a mother who two days after her abortion gave her two five dollar gold pieces to tide her over until she healed, wished her well and left.

She never saw the woman again, although she heard a few years later a woman of her mother's name and description had been brutally tortured and murdered in the Indian Territory just outside Fort Smith. She hoped it was true.

Within days Nettie, one coin in hand and one hidden away, carrying a satchel containing what few possessions she owned, bought a ticket to Ellsworth and shook the dust of Kansas City off her dress tail. Since that time there had been more towns and more men than Nettie Mae could remember. But she always managed to secret away a coin or two into a "sock". She placed great value in "traveling money".

There came times Nettie Mae would allow herself to dream of another life, one without whiskey and men. Her "traveling money" became her dowry at such moments. There was the occasional man, mostly too long and too far from their wives, who treated her with just enough tender mercies to keep the dreams alive. However, the truth was that she had never really had a meaningful conversation with a married woman, and she had long ago accepted the reality that no miracle would bring her a child. Nonetheless, Nettie Mae had her dreams.

Once a customer had tried to steal her "sock" and he got his hand pinned to the night stand by Nettie's knife for his trouble. Nettie Mae's dowry represented too many important elements in her life, of her hopes, to allow anyone to take it.

But now, here on the prairie in the company of two hardworking and focused men who had no carnal interest in her, laying on a bed roll out from under her wagon, gazing at the stars and the bright moon, with the aid of the Chinaman's powder, the discomforts of her illnesses left her. With a level of peace beginning to find her, she drifted off to sleep.

Twenty-Three

C oyote Paw was ambitious for the recognition only gallantry in battle could bring a young Comanche boy. The three wagons, while tightly arranged, were camped well beyond the perimeter of Adobe Walls. This was an inviting and available target. There were no horses and the oxen held no interest, but there were buffalo killers to be slain and the greatest prize of all, a white woman.

The wear upon the white woman made it hard for the boys to determine if she had potential as a captive, or maybe even possessed some trade potential. Nonetheless, there were two white men to kill and scalp, and a white woman.

Eschiti had foretold in his prophecy of a great victory by slaying all the buffalo killers by surprising them in their sleep, still blurred by their whiskey from the night before. While there were no ponies to gain, certainly the first to attack, to bring the scalps of buffalo killers for Eschiti to present to the Great Spirits -- unquestionably that man would be granted great rewards and assigned heroic status.

Coyote Paw had partaken of the potion of the Great Spirits, and was so intoxicated with a conviction of inevitable success that he was beginning to confuse his own ambitions with the guidance of the Great Spirits. In his mind, greatness was the inescapable destiny of Coyote Paw.

So in the early morning darkness, Coyote Paw along with his friend Black Dog's Tongue awakened Toad's Mark, the youngest member of their group, to serve as a horse holder. Coyote Paw sat his pony high and straight as he led his small band from the camp and set out to strike the first blow against the buffalo killers.

The Scheidler campfire glowed dim, but it was clear there was a man sleeping under each of the two front wagons. The woman was sleeping just outside the third.

Coyote Paw and Black Dog's Tongue reached each of the sleeping brothers undetected. But since they did not wish to disturb their potential captive prize, they quickly and silently disposed of the brothers and moved to claim their trophy woman.

Coyote Paw seized Nettie's legs and with his full weight pressed them to the ground before Nettie could even stir.

Nettie Mae quickly assessed the dire nature of her circumstances. She understood there was very limited reason for optimism when it came to her survival. If she screamed, it would be unlikely that the men in Adobe Walls could hear her, and the fresh scalp dripping from Coyote Paw's waist convinced her that her traveling companions were no longer capable of hearing the sound of her voice.

So, Nettie Mae attempted to use her only available resource to tap into the only hope she had, that a lusting male would become a careless male. She lifted her sleeping dress and bunched it around her chest in a way that it revealed only her healthy breast, should the bucks look that high. The night and her heavy pubic hair concealed the several open genital sores that had recently recurred. Maybe, just maybe, this could save her.

Black Dog's Tongue responded to her move by grabbing her wrist and pinning her hands above her head. But Coyote Paw recognized her gesture and cautiously released her feet. Nettie slid her feet back, raising and spreading her knees wide to provide the illusion of a full presentation.

She merged her years of brothel knowledge and experience into a virtuoso performance for her very life.

Coyote Paw threw all caution aside, inebriated by an erotic occurrence for which no previous experience had prepared him. Completed but not done, he simply sat next to Nettie as Black Dog's Tongue rushed through the act, then Nettie Mae again took Coyote Paw between her thighs.

Certain that the boys could not tell the difference between their own deposits and the seepage from her now open and oozing sores, she kept them in passionate embraces until her end finally came.

Coyote Paw galloped into camp, going directly to the morning fire at the outer edge of the camp where Eschiti sat alone. Coyote Paw slid from his pony, and with fresh scalps clutched in his outstretched hands, he strutted toward Eschiti.

Black Dog's Tongue reined up and remained on his pony. While out of the camp's earshot, his reporting of his deeds was adequately animated for all to see the fresh scalps he now held above his head.

Quanah took note of Coyote Paw's arrival. His first concern was that Coyote Paw had revealed their presence to those at the rotting walls so he could take two scalps.

Quanah knew all too well the ambition of youth often provided a fertile breeding ground for stupidity.

But Eschiti stood and reached up so that both he and Coyote Paw held the scalps. Knowing that Coyote Paw's entrance gave him the full attention of those close by, Eschiti declared, "As I, Eschiti prophesied, while they slept. Coyote Paw destroyed the buffalo killers as they slept. *As they slept*! Soon, we shall all sing of the greatness of the coming day and there will be more heroes like Coyote Paw."

Lone Wolf edged next to Quanah. "The scalps are from the men of the wagons with the strange cows."

Quanah shook his head and concurred. "This day has yet to decide its heroes."

Quanah could not have known that the day already had its first hero. While it did not save her life, it was Nettie Mae's cookie that fired the final shots of the first skirmish in the fight at Adobe Walls.

Within a few days, the wounds inflicted by Nettie Mae's weapon of last resort would begin to appear.

Twenty-Four

"Oh, shit!" Startled.

"*Holy shit!!*" Frightened.

*B*illy Ogg had looked up from the water tracing he was creating in the dirt at the base of the tree where he had come to relieve himself. The skyline to the west was covered with movement. While set against the early daybreak sky, they appeared as only slightly more than large dots. He made the dots to be men on horseback, Comanche on horseback forming a line completely across the horizon. The movement of the line gave the illusion it was pulsating, moving toward him and then withdrawing slightly. Then he saw clearly that the line was rapidly advancing toward the makeshift settlement.

Beginning his dash before he had been able to cut off his stream, he wet his pant leg as he made his terrified sprint toward Hanrahan's, now screaming at the top of his lungs, "Comanch, oh shit, Comanch!"

The men gathered in Hanrahan's, as if by fate, were fully awake and alert as they heard the panicked shouts and watched Billy Ogg's wild flight through the entrance of the saloon. These same men had the extreme fine fortune to have been awakened some hours earlier from a deep and for many an alcohol-induced sleep by a cannon-like crack produced by the fracturing of a Cottonwood ridge pole that supported the center section of the roof of Hanrahan's Saloon, giving all below a thorough coating of falling dirt from the quaking sod roof.

The trembling roof sent Dutch Henry and Mike Welch scrambling up the ladder in the front of the saloon, and they quickly begin to remove some of the sod from the stressed area of the roof. Laboring in the dark and not wanting to strain another section of the roof, they carefully stacked the sod pads along the front wall of the store.

The snapped ridge pole brought the camp to a premature awakening and now required that two support post be selected from the stock behind Meyers and Leonard's store. Strong backs struggled to wedge the post into supportive positions.

Then Tommy O'Keefe filled the doorway. With an inconceivably powerful thrust, Tommy guided the post into place with what appeared to be startling ease. The ridge pole was secured.

Dutch and Mike were sitting on the edge of the roof, catching a breath and awaiting the decision about replacing the sod they had just removed and neatly stacked, when they heard and saw Billy Ogg's exhibitionistic dash. In the semi-light of early dawn, they saw the formidable line of hostiles now charging toward them. They lent their voices to Billy Ogg's alarm.

Dixon appeared from O'Keefe's Livery. Tommy closed and barred the heavy wooden doors to the livery as Dixon left. Dixon stepped toward the middle of the street, turning to secure a view of the moving wave of men and horses charging toward him. He carried his Henry in one hand and his .50 caliber Sharps in the other, with two cartridge belts draped across his shoulders.

The Olds, already well into preparing breakfast, dashed past him and into Rath's store.

Dixon discharged his Henry into the air. The report was intended to awakened the final few who might still be sleeping in Rath's and Meyers & Leonard, or those who might have wandered back to their wagons to sleep off the evening in more familiar surroundings.

He discharged a second round and walked toward Hanrahan's.

As he continued his walk toward Hanrahan's, he shouted up to Mike and Dutch to pull the ladder up and stay put. Dixon quickly emerged from Hanrahan's with two Winchester repeaters and a box of cartridges, and carefully pitched them one at a time into Mike and Dutch's waiting hands. Just as Dutch caught the last rifle, an arrow sailed over Dixon's shoulder and took a chip from the adobe. Dixon pushed through the door.

Dutch Henry levered open the Winchester and slapped a cartridge directly into the chamber. His shot was wide, but it distracted the first two horsemen's attention from Dixon's plunge into the Saloon.

He burst right through the door, jarring into Hanrahan with his entrance. Dixon looked at Jim and said, "Think ya shoulda posted a watch?"

"Did. Had ya out there," came Jim's best attempt at a response.

Dixon shrugged and observed, "Good thing Ogg needed a mornin' piss."

Adding, "Heard 'em most all night. Certain that noise come from a pole a'popping?" He turned and began to catalog the men in the saloon before Hanrahan could respond.

The sound of rifle fire from the street interrupted his count. The street in front of the five buildings was now filled with horses and riders. The Indians attacked with every conceivable weapon, from Stone Age lances to bow and arrow to the newest and finest of repeating rifles.

Dixon paused, speaking primarily to himself, "Damn! See 'em sit them ponies!"

His admiration of the Comanche warriors' skill on horseback knew no ethnic boundaries, even in the midst of a pitched fight for survival; a fight that was just underway and was undoubtedly still in question. A stray thought raced through his mind. If old Buck was to get stolen --- the thought broke as a horse crashed into Hanrahan's door. The door held.

"Barricade it! Now!" Jim barked a command. Three men leaped into action, wedging the planks from the tables against the doorway.

Dixon surveyed the group inside the saloon. He turned to Jim and said, "Count three shooters 'sides us. Shooters shoot, all else loads. One on the roof a loader for Dutch?"

Jim agreed. "Ya counted Bat to be a shooter?"

"'Pears he's already shootin'," Dixon said as he moved to join his friend at the small sod opening. There was Masterson, barefooted and still in his long johns, his gun belt fastened around his waist and his black bowler hat sitting atop his head, firing his .44 Colt out the sod opening.

"Damn, backin' their horses into the door." Bat acknowledged Dixon's arrival at the window.

"Just shoot 'em", was Dixon's only reply. "Ogg, ya done pissin' on ya self, come load us."

Hanrahan just shook his head and stepped behind the bar, reached down and produced a shell box containing about 20 "bites", spent .50 caliber shell casings filled with cyanide. He emptied the box on the bar, placed one in his pocket and said nothing. He then took the position next to Bermuda Carlisle at the other window.

Dixon sighted his Henry on a charging brave and dropped him from his pony. Bat leaned to his right, extended his arm out the window and with his .44 Colt shot at a brave trying to back his horse through the door. He missed the warrior but struck the horse in the flank, sending it bolting back into the street. A volley of fire came from Rath's store. Dixon figured three shooters inside.

The first thrust was fierce and all out. Eschiti had designed his plan upon surprise and dim light, to destroy all the buffalo killers while they slept, overwhelming the men at the place of the rotting walls before they could awaken. While not yet organized, the level of lethal fire from the storefront windows exceeded anything Eschiti had foreseen.

Surprise lost, his grand plan deteriorated into a frontal assault on small well-fortified group of experienced marksmen.

Quanah and Howeah again tried to smash through the front door of Hanrahan's Saloon with the rear of their ponies. Pistol shots fired from arms extended out the windows flew by them. As they broke away from the buildings, a bullet struck Howeah in the shoulder, leaving his left arm limp and knocking him into the dust amid the milieu of hooves stirring in the street.

As Howeah tried to arise, Dixon sighted him. Just as Dixon was about to squeeze off the round, Quanah quickly turned his pony and snatched his friend from the street, onto the back of his horse. Dixon tried to adjust his shot on the fly and missed. Quanah carried his friend to safety.

For the next three hours the street of Adobe Walls was constant but indefinable movement, often with more Indians than the street could accommodate. However, while the men inside the buildings grasped that they were locked in a pitched fight for their very lives, they begin to realize that despite being so dramatically outnumbered, if they could hold their barricaded positions the flow of the fight would move toward them. The adobe walls, at most places at least two feet thick, were proving to be impenetrable.

Inside Hanrahan's Saloon, Jim Hanrahan wisely deferred to Dixon's guidance. The soft-spoken Dixon steered the course and Jim barked out the orders. Only the four most skilled shooters were at the windows, windows that were such narrow slits in the sod and adobe that they were virtually firing ports. Dutch, behind the sod escarpment, had an unrestricted line of fire down into the street, and he was taking full advantage of his position.

The window with Bat and Dixon was extraordinarily lethal. Dixon with his Henry and a borrowed Winchester swept the street as Bat's pistols took aim on everything within ten yards of the building. Billy Ogg, a more than decent shot himself, reloaded with both speed and precision.

The other men in the Saloon were loading or reinforcing the barricade at the door. They were opening a hole in the roof where additional cartridges could be passed up to Mike Welch, who was loading for Dutch Henry.

As the efficiency of the firing patterns from Hanrahan's became murderous, Dixon noted the firing from Rath's was erratic except for one window that seemed to be manned by a steady hand. The fire from Myers and Leonard was uneven but steady, although often off target, but nonetheless providing a distracting covering fire limiting full focus on Rath's Store and Hanrahan's Saloon.

It was only when the attackers begin to withdraw that Dixon handed the Henry and the Winchester to Billy Ogg and picked up his Sharps. He handed the rifle up to Jim. Dixon climbed the ladder thru the hole and onto the roof. He reached back and Jim passed him up the Sharps.

Positioned on the roof, he settled his Sharps on its tripod, inserted a cartridge and beaded a retreating Comanche, one of many who felt they were safely out of range and had slowed their ponies, often milling around; appearing to be taunting the buffalo killers.

Dixon cocked the hammer, secured his target, and with a firm steady squeeze released the shot. His shoulder absorbed the stout recoil. The shell struck the rider in the leg with such force that it sent him reeling from his horse. Dixon caressed the stock of the Sharps. He loved the .50 caliber Sharps.

The other Comanche hastened their departure.

Dixon looked at Mike Welch and advised him, "Needed to let' em know we could."

Mike turned and looked behind him. "Damn, burned up Jim's new shitter." The sincere outrage in Mike's voice brought laughter from Dutch, and a smile cracked Dixon's face.

Dixon went back through the hole in the roof. "Jim, think about four Sharps for Dutch and me. Could give 'em doubt. Need a shooter on Rath's roof, too. Better look to what horses ya got left." Dixon caught himself. "Tommy don't need a tellin'"

Jim nodded his agreement. "Got ta move some ammunition over here from Charley's supply. See to it they get a hole in his roof."

Dixon turned to Bat and then looked to Hanrahan. "Jim, Rath stock a few sidearms in that store? Quahadis lookin' at my eyes is fight for sidearms."

Bat took note. He extended his index finger and pushed up the brim of his bowler hat. "Dixon askin' for a handgun. Hell and be damned."

Dixon made a finger gesture directed to Masterson, and Bat had his first good laugh of this day.

Hanrahan reached to the bar and pocketed four of the remaining bites. He looked up and saw Dixon staring at him. "Mrs. Olds is over at Charley's place." Jim made the intent of his actions clear.

With that, Jim and Dixon made a careful dash to Rath's store. James Langton saw the pair coming and swung the door open as they arrived.

Hanrahan placed the bites on the counter, obvious for all to see, but said nothing of them to anyone. Some acts speak adequately loud for themselves, and no man needs to give them voice.

Twenty-Five

*T*he first assault seemingly repelled, Tommy O'Keefe moved out the door of Rath's Store as Hanrahan and Dixon rushed inside. Tears began to well in Tommy O'Keefe's eyes.

Through the smoke of the burning wagons, he could see the dead ponies laying in the street and more injured ones confused and wandering in aimless pain, not understanding the nature of their plight. Tommy was the first to fully step out onto the street. He focused upon a Paint mare bleeding from a gunshot wound to her hip. She remained standing by what Tommy assumed to be the Paint's now deceased owner.

Tommy gently took the buckskin bridle and rubbed her muzzle. He opened the heavy wooden doors to the livery and led the pony inside.

Billy Tyler watched from inside Rath's, then inexplicably beyond his innate affection for horses stepped outside and began to help Tommy round up other ponies that appeared rather uninjured.

Tommy used his smith tools to probe for shells, used his hot irons, his balms and salves to seal the wounds and bring some temporary relief. An intermittent revolver shot from outside told him of the fate of other ponies.

As he was done with each pony that Billy now brought to him, he'd lay the head of the pony upon his shoulder, rub it and turn the pony loose into his unbreeched stockade corral. Now his compassion was giving way to simple rage as he peered out upon the dead animals in street. Tommy was a smith and ran a livery because he loved the animals. He deeply loved the animals.

Now missing Billy Tyler, and not seeing him in the street, Tommy stepped up into the hayloft and peered out the window across the meadow. He saw Billy intent on getting a rope around a slightly hobbled bay mare. He had pursued her a distance beyond the relatively safety of Adobe Walls, well beyond earshot, although Tommy shouted for him to come back.

Four of the Kiowa braves who rode with Lone Wolf suddenly appeared from the tree line. Billy was so intent upon securing the mare, they were upon him before he saw them.

Quickly drawing his revolver from his belt, Billy unseated the Kiowa closest to him and moved the now secure mare between him and the charging Kiowas. The first shot from the Kiowas dropped the mare where she stood. Billy managed to get off another shot before the Kiowas completely overran him. One of the next two shots certainly killed Billy, but warriors shot him several more times before dismounting and scalping him.

The roar of the Sharps from Rath's roof sent the Kiowas back into the tree line. Tommy looked closely for any sign of movement from Billy, but none came.

The stories from his Scottish mother of the Scots and Pics repelling the invading Romans renewed themselves in Tommy's mind. Deeply hurt and increasingly filled with a righteous anger, he begin what he felt to be a ritual preparation to ready himself for battle, to defend the horses in his livery and behind the walls of his reinforced stockade corral.

By the time the next charge came about an hour later, Tommy O'Keefe, naked except for his leather smith's apron and now transfigured by a coating of wood ash and water, was prepared to protect the animals in his care. He left one of the massive doors cracked open and positioned himself.

Tommy's trap was set.

Twenty-Six

"Done gotta hole in the roof," Langton told Hanrahan as Dixon's attention immediately went to the shelves.

The stockpile of cartridges and rifles caught both Dixon's eye and his imagination. "Damn, Jim, ol' Charley might a left us, but he left us armed."

Not only was the opening onto the roof of Rath's completed, but Andy Johnson, a hunter who was awakened by Dixon's shots in the street and found refuge in the closest place to his wagon, had already taken a position on the rear of the structure, providing him with a clear line of fire as far as the tree line on the creek. But none of the horses that had been grazing in the meadow before the initial onslaught remained. Lone Wolf's warriors had been most efficient in clearing the meadow of the horses while the buffalo killers had been fighting off the first attack.

Andy the Swede looked back to William Olds, whose head was just poking through the opening, and said, "Tell Jim I got a good sightin' but ain't many horses left to watch over."

Olds relayed the message. Andy could hear Hanrahan's response. "Tell that damn Swede I ain't plannin' on takin' no ride soon." Andy and Olds both chuckled. Jim muttered to himself, "Hell, my animal's with Tommy anyways."

Hannah Olds, contemplating the nature of men, turned back to her window and smiled.

Dixon stepped away from the gun racks and said, "Look here. .44 caliber Sharps. Still in its wrappins'." He admired it before adding, "Didn't know of such a thing."

Jim and Dixon continued filling two totes with cartridges, mostly .44 caliber. Dixon took note that it was Hannah Olds who seemed to be manning the window from where the effective fire had seemed to have been coming.

Bags filled, he walked to the window. "Mrs. Olds, ya been the shooter here?" She smiled without opening her lips as she nodded in the affirmative.

"My gramps said I'd a knack."

"Ma'am, I'd rightly agree with ya gramps."

He removed his hat and put it on her head, then started re-loading his Henry. Half-turning to Jim, who had moved beside them, he spoke, "Just as soon them hostiles not figure there be a woman here, if they don't know."

Jim twitched his mouth and nodded his agreement. Hannah Olds tied her hair back and adjusted the hat to her head.

"Jim, you got plenty of shooters in your place. I'll be stayin' here," Dixon stated. "Looks like really just Andy and the lady guardin' all this powder. Eddy can help ya carry."

"If the breed figures out we got this many guns and a woman, he'll not be as foolish as he was a bit ago. He'll come all holy hell after this place," Jim observed.

"Suspect the mornin' was the holy man stew, tain't Quanah's way," Dixon responded.

"Maybe," came the answer.

"Jim, tell Masterson to glance this way from time to time."

"Yep, I will."

Twenty-Seven

*A*fter leading the first thrust against the buffalo killers, Quanah dismounted in the tree line near the creek. The bullets and arrows were not piercing the sod and adobe. The chinked cottonwood walls appeared vulnerable. But the doors were stout and had withstood repeated charges by horses. Quanah felt what he had suspected from the onset was being confirmed.

He was coming to understand victory must be redefined. Victory is not determined by destroying "The Rath" and killing all of the buffalo killers. Victory must be seen in the number of their horses that could be taken and burning their wagons, by delaying their prompt return to the prairie and allowing the buffalo herds to pass unharmed.

Eschiti still controlled the hopes, the hearts and the minds of far too many, but as more young men fell to the bullets of the buffalo killers, belief in his magic would fade. Quanah could wait, he could lead with courage, but the Nermernuh must survive to fight battles they could win.

The Quahadis were superior on the open plains. There an attack on the white man was analogous to a buffalo hunt. But a frontal attack as Eschiti spoke of in his prophecies could not end well. Not against barricaded marksmen.

Lone Wolf came alongside Quanah. "The medicine of Eschiti is dung and dirt."

"Worse," Quanah allowed. "His vision of battle is flawed. The buffalo killers shoot like a Quahadis rides – and some Kiowa – and the rotting walls protect them better than Eschiti's potion protects our warriors."

After a pause, giving Lone Wolf the chance to add his thoughts, Quanah continued. "If we come from the sides, fewer guns can shoot at us until we are before the stores. If we fire all the wagons of the Rath, the smoke might hinder their eyes."

Howeah, his arm now bandaged, rode up to the pair and announced, "Eschiti says that we must charge again, that we failed the first time because a Kiowa killed a skunk on our way to the rotting walls."

Lone Wolf was outraged. "Ask my dead warriors about the wisdom of Eschiti." Lone Wolf launched a handful of dirt toward Howeah and pointed toward Adobe Walls, saying, "I fight to kill them. Not for the glory of Eschiti." Gesturing toward Quanah, he said, "I fight beside my friend."

Howeah backed away and said, "I tell you what Eschiti said. And Quanah is more than my friend. He saved me this morning. I too fight beside my friend."

Lone Wolf tossed a second handful of dirt into the air. "I do not like this place."

Quanah, attempting to reframe the definition of victory remarked, "Lone Wolf captured their pony herd, a herd of many fine ponies, and that is a good thing." He paused and thoughtfully added, "We must fire every wagon that is not already burning."

His true thought was that it was too bad that the adobe structures with their sod roofs wouldn't burn.

Twenty-Eight

"*H*ostiles! Comin' again!" Andy shouted out from the roof, then fired a shot toward a passing cloud.

Jim Hanrahan and George Eddy made a dash out the door and for the Saloon. The sound of Dutch Henry's voice now cursing the second could be heard atop Hanrahan's Saloon.

There was no surprise this time. As the wave of horsemen descended, using the whitewashed tree as a marker, Dutch Henry, Billy Ogg, and Mike Welch roared to life. Each now had three Sharps 50's laying beside them on the roof tops. The sound of the Sharps being fired in volley sequence crashed up the slope with a thunderous roar. The volleys were deadly, but they were nothing compared to the all-out fire of the repeating rifles that greeted the charging hostiles as they passed the whitewashed 180-yard tree marker.

Nonetheless, the wave of horsemen surged forward, back into the streets of Adobe Walls. As they approached the buildings, a wave of pistol fire erupted. At such close range, it was now a fight to be won by the pistol.

William Olds scrambled from the roof and had begun to descend the ladder when his rifle discharged. The bullet entered beneath his chin and exited the top of his head. He was dead when he hit the floor of Rath's Store.

Hannah turned at the sound of the shot to see her husband slam into the floor. Although she didn't, she appeared to reach him and embrace his head before it could strike the floor. Tears flooded from her eyes and she rocked his head as one would rock a baby. The hushed sounds that escaped her mouth had more the sound of a lullaby than of the moans that would have more accurately expressed the depth of her grief. But those sounds of sadness reached no ears other than hers, her mournful cries being absorbed into the clamor of horses and men and gunfire.

In the midst of the bedlam of battle, she cradled his head and brushed his hair with her hand until a bullet crashed into the ladder, splintering the ladder rung.

A Comanche warrior had positioned himself in the window Hannah vacated as her William fell. Hannah bolted upright, fearful the warrior would further injure her husband, and turned toward the window. She seized her Winchester and stood. She took solid aim at the window as the warrior fired again, missing his target. Hannah's shot struck him square, knocking him back from the window.

As another hostile immediately appeared, Hannah levered in another cartridge and shot him dead. With measured steps, steadying her rifle after each recoil, Hannah Olds shot her way back to the window, progressively levering in a new round and firing. There was no jerk in her trigger finger, just a smooth steady squeeze as each compression of the trigger unleashed a destructively precise shot.

Hannah Olds retook the window she had abandoned when William fell.

Dixon turned to Langdon. "Be damn, didya see! Miss Hannah's walk to the window! Damn! Go load her."

With Jim Langdon reloading her rifles and tears pouring down her cheeks, with sobs her only sounds, Hannah Olds laid a savage barrage into the street until the barrel of one Winchester became so hot it jammed. Jim took it from her, handed her another and set the overheated repeating rifle aside.

Twenty-Nine

*T*ommy O'Keefe heard Andy Johnson's voice as if it rang from the mountainsides and through the glens of Scotland, sounding the alarm of this second charge. In the depths of his soul, he heard the wail of the pipes. Now transfigured into the Scottish-Irish warrior of his grandmother's tales, he prepared to protect the animals in his care. He lay in wait behind the cracked door of temptation, positioned atop the wall of the first stall, just above the height of a man on horseback.

To the frustration of the ever-ambitious Coyote Paw, still basking in the glow of his great victory at the Scheidler wagons, White Hawk spotted the slightly open livery door first and led the charge toward the opening. White Hawk, exuberant with his coup over Coyote Paw, smashed through the door of the livery.

Tommy O'Keefe stood astride the stall, clad only by ash and his leather smith's apron, tightening his grip on his short hand sledge. With a single swing, he struck the charging White Hawk full in the forehead. The warrior's head exploded like a July watermelon, spewing bone and brains over Tommy. Coyote Paw and Runs Like Walking froze, their bodies stiffening in the manner only great terror can induce, the sensation that limbs have become so heavy that they cannot be moved.

O'Keefe, with a high leap, dismounted the railing and stood in front of the warriors, warriors who had just seen their companion's head disappear from atop his body. Now in front of them stood this massive figure, biceps bulging with his hammer in one hand and a pitchfork in the other, his face reddened beneath the ashes by rage and splatters of blood. Draped across his balding head and trailing down his forehead were two strands of what had until recently been White Hawk's brain.

The sight before them produced a paralyzing terror like nothing they had ever experienced before. Although O'Keefe made no move toward them, rather standing as the stoic guardian, they fled the livery in an explosive panic. As they fled, Tommy launched his pitch fork. The pitch fort struck Runs Like Walking with such impact that he was knocked to the ground writhing in pain, but prevented from turning over by the handle of the pitch fork. He lay face down in the dust just beyond the livery doors.

Thomas O'Keefe stood guard at the doorway of his livery like the Colossus protecting the island of Rhodes, hammer in his right hand with both immense arms reaching toward the sky.

Coyote Paw realized the demon of the devil was not pursuing him. He jumped from his pony, pulled the pitch fork from Runs Like Walking's back and boosted him across the back of his pony.

At that point, O'Keefe loosed a roar from so deep in his chest that it sounded as if it reached back to his ancestors who, naked with their bodies painted blue, had come storming from the hills of Scotland to repel the Roman invaders.

The raw fierceness of the sound made Coyote Paw give up any thoughts of turning his pony toward the livery in a gesture of defiance, an act he might have later claimed as a coup against the mighty hammer swinger of the rotting walls. With Runs Like Walking draped across his pony, Coyote Paw drove his heels into his pony, sending the animal sprinting back toward the open plains.

Tommy lifted White Hawk by the feet and pulled him from the livery into the street. He stared toward the fleeing pair and dropped White Hawk's feet to the ground.

Tommy O'Keefe closed and barred the livery doors.

Thirty

I n repelling the second major thrust against Adobe Walls, it only took a look at the carnage in the street to realize that there was now a clear tide to fight. The adobe walls of the buildings were filled with pock marks where large chips had been knocked from them by the almost six hours of incoming bullets.

Dixon was the first to step into the street. He simply shook his head.

"God almighty!" It was the only phase that would slide through Jim Hanrahan's lips as he got his first glimpse at the carnage in the street. "Good God almighty!"

"Olds is dead. No hostile got him, just damn misfortune." The information was directed toward Bat, who had now joined them. Dixon's audible appreciation continued. "Ya shoulda see'd Miss Hannah's walk. Sight ta behold."

Dixon directed their sight to the six Indian bodies that were outside her window. "Comanch don't leave their dead easy," he again added with unabashed admiration. "By God, ya shoulda seen her."

As the others made their way from the buildings, they begin to move without being instructed. They were hunters, skinners or teamsters. They needed no instructions about dead animals and how to clear them from the street. Although the raiders had retrieved many of their dead from the street as the fight had raged on, seven Comanche and Kiowa men lay dead in the street, along with the six clustered by the window of Mrs. William Olds.

The smell of a day of death, of the pungent effectiveness of a day in the west Texas sun on the carcasses of Indian and animal, did not impair those accustomed to the buffalo hunt. They went about the necessary business of clearing the street with little instruction as to the need for the task or how to undertake it.

In this panorama of death, it was only a glimpse at what Tommy's hammer had done to White Hawk that gave these frontiersmen even the slightest pause.

The merchants among them were something of a different story. But no man shirked his obligation.

The water barrels were refilled from Hanrahan's well. Food was distributed from Myers and Leonard's Store.

The Scheidler brothers' four surviving oxen were fed and watered, then pressed into service to pull the dead animals out a couple of hundred yards onto the plains, but to an area that always gave Mike and Dutch a clear line of sight. Although quite sun-burned and dehydrated by an already full day on the roof, they talked and drank from a water bucket that had been passed up to them. Still their eyes never neglected the ridge or the tree line.

William Olds and Billy Tyler were cleaned and wrapped in canvas and buried in individual graves near a small grove of hackberry trees just west of Myers and Leonard's store. Their graves were appropriately deep and suitably marked. Mrs. William Olds saw to it all was conducted as proper as conditions allowed.

Jacob and Isaac Scheidler, along with Nettie Mae, were buried in a shallower common grave by the remains of the brothers' burned wagons. The Scheidler brothers were buried with their dreams. Miss Nettie Mae was buried with her dowry of gold stitched into the reinforced bodice of her dress.

And some wondered why Miss Nettie Mae wasn't mutilated as the brothers were.

One of the men remarked, "Guess livin' cut her up aplenty."

Another concurred, "Likely so."

Some care was taken to level out the ground and then cover the site with the charred remains of the wagons.

There was considerable discussion about the dead warriors. Dixon was insistent that they be taken out a safe distance and left. But there was considerable opposition, led by several extremely vocal dissenters, some of whom wanted to remove the warrior's heads and place them upon stakes across the path the hostiles had used on the first attack.

As the disagreement intensified, Jim Hanrahan fired his pistol into the air and ended the discussion. "Lost my brother in the War and didn't get ta bury him proper. Still gnaws at my gut. We'll be sendin' these to their kin."

The tone of Jim's voice alone would have likely quelled the most passionate challenger, but when Hannah Olds, her dusty face still marked by the path of her tears and fresh from burying William, stepped alongside Jim, any discussion ended.

As they moved from earshot, Dixon said, "Didn't know ya had a brother in the war."

"Didn't," was the reply. "Don't want to give the Comanch cause to stay longer 'n need be."

Dixon fully understood. "Goin' ta find a bit of white cloth."

"Comanch get that?"

"Quanah does."

The bodies of the fallen warriors, all neatly facing the same direction, were place upon a wagon tarp. The tarp was hooked to two oxen.

Dixon walked out onto the prairie beside two oxen, dragging the body-laden tarp. He escorted the bodies of the dead warriors out past the whitewashed tree. There Dixon unhitched the oxen and left the men to be claimed by their people during the safety of the night.

The concentrated effort to remove the remains of the day was completed with a remarkable stillness.

By sunup, the men had been claimed. The empty tarp rustled in the morning breeze.

Thirty-One

A bone-tired Quanah eased into his seat by the fire, waiting for the gathering that would inevitably occur. His wait was not long. Several others quickly joined him.

Lone Wolf came from a gathering of Kiowa and seated himself next to Quanah. He spoke softly. "Many of my brothers will be leaving this cause. They will speak of needing to go and join the Sun Dance upstream from the Medicine Lodge. They fear that they might have fallen from favor by taking the potion of Eschiti. They will leave at daybreak and will not fight tomorrow."

Quanah asked, "And Lone Wolf?"

"Lone Wolf and some others will choose to stay. I fight the buffalo killers. It is their leaders and their medicine that desires to take the life that belongs to us. Our children must be Kiowa, Comanche and Cheyenne."

"My friend, we must fight, but we cannot fight until we are no more. There must be Kiowa and Comanche, or there will be no children," Quanah said, waiting briefly before continuing, "We must fight the white man as we hunt the buffalo. We must fight this fight where we can win, in the open grasses of our plains and not in places like the rotting walls."

"Quanah, the blue coats may now come deeper into our lands. They no longer make war with each other."

"Perhaps," Quanah acknowledged his shared concern. "But our grass lands are large. And we can find them more easily than they can find us."

"I know your wisdom. It saddens me that you may be right. You must know others feel that no matter how brave you are in battle, there is paleness in your heart." Lone Wolf spoke his mind.

Again, Quanah asked, "And Lone Wolf?"

Lone Wolf was thoughtful, then answered, "Our future might be best in the hands of one who understands the white man." He paused. "But I cannot yet come to like the thought."

Although that response gave rise to more questions than it provided answers in Quanah's mind, he spoke no further of the matter, simply stating, "I will not speak by the council fire tonight."

They sat quietly, each lost in his visions of the future, until the council circle had formed.

Eschiti opened the council. He stood holding a jar of his potion before him. He said, "The life source promised by the Great Spirits escaped from the potion when a Kiowa killed a skunk on our way to the place of the rotting walls."

Eschiti, as with most of the camp, knew the Kiowa no longer believed in the medicine of Eschiti and were leaving at daybreak for the large Sun Dance near the Medicine Lodge. Eschiti did not mind irritating the Kiowa.

Outraged, Kicking Bird leapt to his feet. "The Kiowa shall leave for the true medicine of the Sun Dance at the Medicine Lodge."

Kicking Bird left the circle. But Lone Wolf only moved a few paces away and turned with arms crossed, staring at Eschiti. It was clear to all present that despite his distaste for Eschiti, Lone Wolf was not leaving this fight. Lone Wolf's hate for the white man exceeded his disgust with Eschiti and his false medicine.

"Coyote Paw tells of a powerful and fearful warrior who protects the ponies at the place at the rotting walls, a warrior whose black paint is more powerful than the potion of Eschiti. Eschiti's potion did not protect White Hawk today," said Prairie Wolf's in a voice carrying his anger and sense of betrayal.

A pained voice from the dark pierced the circle. "My youngest son, Chases Rabbits, died in the dirt of the place of the rotting walls today. He was a believer, but the bullets from the behind the rotting walls tore through the very spot his potion was painted."

A greater truth had just been spoken. Many of the warriors who now fought were hardly more than children. This truth resonated throughout the gathering. Eschiti could offer no words to console a grieving father who had lost a son, a son who just a boy.

"Best Son In Law is dead. He was left in the dust and would spend this night there, had the Dirty Hat not returned him to me. He should not have been left," another anguished and angry voice came from the dark.

The anger in the voice grew. "He should not have been left!"

Eschiti raised his voice, hoping to redirect the anger, and said, "The Dirty Hat moved our dead with the strange cows. He disrespected our dead."

Though it had not been his intention to speak, never rising and in his firmest and most direct voice, Quanah did speak. "The Dirty Hat did not leave our dead in the dust. He walked beside the strange cows and pulled them to us. The Dirty Hat is a warrior and he revered our dead. A warrior returned our warriors. Tomorrow I may kill him, but I will not speak ill of him this night."

Eschiti immediately grasped this was not a tide of emotion that was flowing in his favor, and he had not words to turn it.

"I, Eschiti, must go to the river and watch the running waters for a sign to pass with the currents. The Great Spirits will not abandon us just because a Kiowa killed a skunk. But we were sent to prove ourselves worthy of buffalo. I will seek forgiveness for the skunk so the Great Spirits will know that we have not betrayed them. Perhaps the killing of the skunk was a part of the design of the Great Spirits to further test our conviction. Yes, I see that the skunk was meant to tempt the Nermernuh and not our Kiowa brothers." A conciliatory remark uttered far too late. "I, Eschiti, believe in the running waters the Great Spirits will reveal the path to fulfill the task assigned us by the Great Spirits to bring back the buffalo and banish victory."

The bones were tired, the day had been long, and most distressing of all, even Eschiti's most zealous of believers had begin to doubt he had brought them invincibility from the bullets of the buffalo killers. But despite great evidence to the contrary, there are times in the lives of all men when they will cling to hope beyond all reason, because what the hope offers is so personally valuable. For the Nermernuh, this was a time for such desperate hopefulness.

Quanah and Lone Wolf knew that soon, those with the unwavering resolve to fight and achieve victories would come to them. Let Eschiti go look into the muddy waters of the flowing river to the south. Time would allow the inevitable to become evident. Quanah and Lone Wolf were reluctantly arriving at the understanding victory might only be found in survival for the Nermernuh and the Kiowa.

Although he attempted a somewhat ceremonial exit, Eschiti departed the camp almost unacknowledged.

Thirty-Two

*A*t daybreak, all of the Kiowa, except for the twenty or so who chose to ride with Lone Wolf, left their campsite and began their trek toward the Medicine Lodge to join the Sun Dance.

The mood of the camp was somber. Eschiti was gone and seeking guidance in the rusty water of the Red River. Quanah and Lone Wolf chose to let those men linger aimlessly around the morning fires, thinking on the time of Eschiti's return, wondering what wisdom could stop the buffalo killers' bullets or penetrate the thick adobe walls that protected them.

Small disorganized groups would leave the camp and fire at the small settlement from a safe distance. Only the sound of the shots reached Adobe Walls.

One group made a half-hearted charge that sent the defenders of Adobe Walls to their now organized firing positions. The only real shots were simply diversions for attempts to steal what few horses were still wandering in the meadow between Adobe Walls and the creek.

The men at Adobe Walls had awakened to the pleasing and comforting smells of coffee, hot yeast bread and frying buffalo meat. Old Man Keeler, having lived long enough to bury many of his own kin, was sensitive to Mrs. Olds' circumstances and to what might help them all on this morning. There was no balm for the exhausted body and weary soul like the fragrance of familiar foods being prepared and the sounds that accompany its preparation.

It was these smells and sounds that brought Hannah Olds alert, like answering a fire bell. She left the pall of death and came to her kitchen. She returned to her pots and pans, to the sounds of her life. The cooking occupied Hannah's thoughts and feeding hungry men still warmed her. It gave her the knowledge that despite death, life still lurked inside her.

Never leaving the horizon unwatched, the men came into Eats in small bunches, friends engaging in conversations and telling tales of the day before and speaking of tomorrows. Little can reinvigorate men like conversation shared over a table of good food.

Having been surrounded by death and desolation until the late hours of the previous evening, the well-fed men found a renewal of spirit in the talk over a second cup of fresh coffee on Charley Rath's round tables.

As a group, the assemblage at Adobe Walls had liked and respected Mr. and Mrs. Olds. This meal gave them a chance to express their genuine condolences to Hannah. She found their often awkward but sincere expressions of reverence for her loss to be genuinely touching. She found comfort in the softened sounds now made by ordinarily gruff men, but it was Dixon, Stetson in hand, who spontaneous leaned forward and delicately kissed her cheek that brought tears to her eyes.

Hannah turned away, looked up and thought to her husband, "Well, William, you got a proper Wake after all."

Then, she wiped the tears from the corners of her eyes and allowed herself to feel twinges of life returning to the core of her being.

Quanah and Lone Wolf slowly worked their way along the tree line of the creek, seeking a point of attack should the sandy river tell Eschiti another frontal assault upon the rotting walls was the path to victory. They sought a place where warriors could exhibit their bravery and not have to die for their gallant displays.

The scent of coffee and frying meat caught Quanah's nose. He shook his head at Lone Wolf and said, "Our enemy does not suffer."

"The white man cooks with too many smells." This was Lone Wolf's conclusion.

Quanah did not tell his Kiowa comrade that the food was the only good memory he had of his time in the Texas place.

By dusk, Eschiti had yet to return. The second day ended as quietly as it had begun.

Thirty-Three

S hortly before mid-day, word came to the camps that Eschiti
had returned and that he awaited atop the crest that
overlooked the place of the rotting walls. Quanah, Lone Wolf,
Big Tree, Howeah and Yellow Fish mounted and rode to the crest
of one of the rolling hills overlooking the place of the rotting
walls to hear what the Great Spirits had revealed to Eschiti in the
swirling waters of the river.

They became annoyed as they discovered Eschiti's plan to
destroy the place of the rotting walls was little changed. As
Quanah and Lone Wolf spoke their disagreement more openly,
the gathering became contentious. Howeah kept his silence. As
Eschiti found that he had no real supportive allies remaining in
leadership, he became more animated, insisting on a larger
forum, still convinced he could sway many warriors.

Mike Welch was the first to spot the gathering on the distant
crest. He shouted down to the Swede who was coming from the
saloon toward Rath's, "Tell Dixon some hostiles on the hill.
Might wanta see if he can."

"Be up." It was Dixon who had just stepped onto the street,
his Sharps in one hand and his Henry in the other with a sidearm
in his belt, headed toward Hanrahan's, who replied.

Billy Ogg now on the roof with Welch, added his
observation. "Ah, he's funnin' with ya. Good mile to 'em."

"Be up," Dixon responded.

He stepped into the saloon and found Jim. "Ya got a couple
of ya big 50's?"

Hanrahan reached beneath the bar and retrieved two
cartridges. "Extra loads. Have fun." Dixon retrieved his
binoculars from his bag, sat his Henry on the bar and made his
way up the ladder.

"Hot damn, I say he hits somethin'." Billy Ogg voiced his
brash support and admiration of Dixon.

Now atop the roof, Dixon saw the group of what appeared
to be hostiles milling about near the crest of a hill about three

quarters of a mile or so away. He took out his binoculars and peered toward the hill, slowly sweeping the group.

Dixon carefully placed his binoculars to the side and began to move some of the sod that had been stacked along the edge of the roof. He laid his Stetson to the side and took a prone position on the roof, then placed the barrel of the Sharps on a tripod. Dixon cradled the stock snugly into his right shoulder. While the prone firing position was comfortable, there was something in the extension of his left arm and the feel against his cheek and his eyes sighting down the barrel while his body literally relaxed into the firing position that seemed to bring all the pieces of Dixon's world into unison. His right hand pulled the hammer back toward the cocked position. The sound of each click brought the confidence and reassurance of the familiar. With a smooth steady pressure on the trigger, he released the power of the rifle. The explosion in the chamber brought a remarkable sensation that penetrated the very soul of Billy Dixon.

The recoil literally knocked Dixon backward, despite the sod of the roof. Frenchy and the Swede cupped their ears in response to the roar.

"*Hit one*! By damn, he hit one," exclaimed Ogg. Welch's mouth fell open, gaping in disbelief.

Despite the forceful recoil, Dixon's eyes were stationary, looking out over the barrel toward his now fallen target. He rose to one knee, still looking toward the hill, and said, "Dropped him."

He picked up his binoculars and started toward the ladder.

"Ain't ya gonna look?" Ogg inquired. Beyond Dixon, there was just general amazement at the shot.

Pulling the mid of his lips upward, Dixon shook his head no.

To the men on the roof, the ponies on the hill appeared to be circling in a rather erratic manner the spot where the man had appeared to fall, and then retreated in a disorderly fashion until they left the sight of the men on the roof.

Yellow Tail would never be certain if he first saw the puff of smoke or heard the loud and implausible thud as the bullet struck Eschiti in the shoulder, completely unseating him from his pony. But he did know that both occurred before the sound of the shot reached his ears. This was a sensation he found most disquieting. As such stories are prone to do, the interval of time between Eschiti being struck and the arrival of the shot that dropped him expanded.

Quanah stared down at Eschiti, whose left arm was virtually severed from his shoulder. At first he gazed in disbelief. Then, the relief one feels knowing that a foe had been struck by providence, and maybe the Great Spirits had intervened. Dead or not, Eschiti was no longer the invincible rival possessed of great magic and mysticism.

As Quanah rode away alongside Howeah and Lone Wolf, the thought of divine intervention became more plausible to him. He uttered his thought. "The Great Spirits have spoken."

Lone Wolf locked eyes with Quanah. "Dirty Hat."

Quanah nodded. "Dirty Hat."

Lone Wolf added to his thoughts. "Rotting walls was not a good place for a fight. The buffalo killers do not die easily there."

In less than an hour, the stories were told, camps were broken and the attackers left the place of the rotting walls, each to fight again on another day, to fight in another way.

Quanah rode back for a view of the place, paused as if preserving in his mind a place he did not intend to revisit, but knew he should never forget. He turned his pony, and with the wind at his back he spit toward Adobe Walls, then he left.

Thirty-Four

*B*at Masterson was already enjoying the late afternoon shade of the cottonwood and the empty horizon to the west, sitting with his back against the adobe wall of Myers and Leonard's Store. Dixon took a seat on the ground next to his friend. Dixon took off his Stetson, surveyed it and then placed it on his knee.

"Didn't think ya could get that thing any dirtier, but damn if ya didn't," Masterson observed. Dixon raised his lips at the left corner, moving them in what passed for a smile.

They sat quietly, Dixon smoking his cob pipe and sipping a glass poured from Jim Hanrahan's private supply. Masterson coughed trying to inhale Haranhan's gift cigar, and looked westward toward the ridge line.

A lusty roar erupted from Hanrahan's establishment. Reports sounded as two revolver loads were discharged.

Masterson said, "Hell, if Jim don't shut off that damn free whiskey soon, boys gonna do to each other what Quanah and his Quahadis bucks couldn't do."

When no immediate response came from Dixon, he looked toward his companion. Bat's off-handed comment had given Dixon a momentary pause.

"Quanah woulda fought it different," he said. Then, thinking back on the fight, he concluded, "Need ta get me a better sidearm."

As if completely synchronized with the musings of his friend, Bat agreed, "Pistols win if the fightin's up snug."

Continuing to look at the grasslands, never turning toward Masterson, Dixon again surveyed the hat sitting on his knee, seeming to check the brim, lifted it close to his face. Mrs. Hannah's fragrance had faded, but its memory was still pleasant. And then he spoke.

"Old Priest come all the way from Santa Fe to Fort Sumner to visit me. Wanted to know this land. To Sumner in a buckboard 'cause some hunter told I'd know about this land. Priest says he came from Spain lots of years ago. I suppose he did, but mostly sounded Mexican to me. Don't know I'd know a difference. Said he shipped to Galveston and with some other folks come across part of the Llano, must been south of Palo Dura, getting to Santa Fe."

Dixon paused before going on. Masterson would have usually jumped into such an opening in the conversation, but he was somewhat taken back, not realizing that his friend could string together that many words, much less that he could talk that long at a time.

"He showed me an old map he'd drawed after he made Santa Fe. Left the Llano empty. Almost from San Anton' to Santa Fe. You know what he wrote at the edges?"

Not waiting for an answer, Dixon continued. "Wrote 'Here Be Dragons'. Said that was what old time map drawers would write at the edges of the world."

Unable to contain his tongue any longer, Masterson said, "I'll bet that old Priest knew about the Comanch."

Now Dixon turned his head and stared at Masterson. "Or 'haps he heard enough church confessings that knew about us. Comanch is mean mad and what they done to Whistlin' Charley – and likely'll do lots of other folks 'fore this is done -- ain't right. But I hear officer talk. The soldier boys protect us hiders so we'll kill off the buffalo – and well, Comanch that don't get killed get prodded to them reservations places. Or starve with no buffalo."

"Bat, don't know who be the dragons. 'Haps its us." Dixon was thoughtful before adding, "If the grass could talk it'd say we all be dragons to this land."

The thought left both speaker and listener in silence until Dixon again spoke. "Surely do like this land."

After a pause, Bat offered his view. "I have trouble findin' much to like. Think I'll find me a town I like and stay in it a while."

"I'll be here," was Dixon's response. "Thinkin' on dragons."

Another series of loud cries came from Haranhan's as a fight spilled out the door and onto the dusty street. A single shot sounded.

The sun began to set.

Thirty-Five

*H*is camp now some distance away, Quanah sat covered by a blanket gazing into a campfire. He abruptly pulled himself upright as if he heard a disquieting sound in the distance, or perhaps an unsettling vision. He squinted into the coming darkness, seeking even a glimpse. His right arm relaxed and his hand held the peyote pipe by his side.

He knew he must consult the walls of the Palo Duro for the wisdom of his ancestors. He must sit by the fire with Weakeah, eat from the Mexican bowl and come to experience peace so that he might come to more fully understand it. He hoped peace brought comfort and warmth, like being under the robes of morning with Weakeah.

He sought a future that gave the Nermernuh a place in a land that had always belonged to them. A way the Nermernuh might exist with the quarrelsome and possessive white man. How do you trust the man who appears driven to steal or to destroy what is yours?

Even in the midst of such great ambiguity, Quanah recognized the inevitable. It was his conviction that on the ledges of the Canyon, filled with the wisdom of his ancestors with the peyote pipe and in the robes of morning with Weakeah, answers would come. He missed his wife and her soft counsel.

Near a small cluster of red cedars at the edge of the camp, Coyote Paw winched at the painful, burning urination that had began adding to the discomfort of the itching that had bothered him the past few days. The cloudy fluid now seeping from the tip of his penis puzzled him.

Black Dog's Tongue saw him standing in the cedars and walked over. After a brief exchange, the movements of his own body appeared to indicate his understanding. Black Dog's Tongue scratched at an itch beneath his loin cloth as he walked away.

The Dragons belched their fire. The Elephant swished his tail and drifted into the night until he was no more, leaving a trail into the darkness for the buffalo to follow.

Then, just for a moment, the evening breeze settled.

Part Five

Buffalo Wallow
September 1874

Thirty-Six

*T*he Red River War, the climatic campaign against the tribes of the southern plains, was well under way. Billy Dixon found himself once again scouting for the United States Calvary. At the encouragement of Amos Chapman, he had enlisted to serve under Colonel Nelson Appleton Miles with the Sixth Cavalry.

On September 10, 1874, a supply train coming for Camp Supply in the Indian Territory, under the command of Captain Wyllys Lyman, had not arrived in what Colonel Miles considered to be a timely fashion. The shortage of supplies was delaying the now quite impatient Colonel Miles from sustaining his pursuit of the Comanche as they were withdrawing toward the Palo Duro country.

He preferred to engage them on the open prairie rather than entrenched in the Palo Duro Canyon. And he certainly did not relish the idea of a winter campaign.

The truth was the Colonel sought a clear and decisive victory from which he could emerge again a hero. In the United States Army of 1874, the glow of his highly deserved Medal of Honor for gallantry at Chancellorsville was dimming. While he was considered successful, there was the persistent whispering in the ranks that his marriage to the niece of General William Tecumseh Sherman brought him unmerited favors. Such rumors irritated and drove this veteran of every major battle in the Civil War except Gettysburg.

Unbeknownst to Colonel Miles, Captain Lyman and his supply train were under siege near the Washita River by a group of Kiowa and Comanche warriors fighting alongside Lone Wolf and Satanta.

Colonel Miles sent his aide to fetch Sergeant Zachariah T. Woodall and two civilian scouts, Amos Chapman and Billy Dixon.

Sergeant Woodall, who had risen in rank during the Civil War and unlike many had rapidly adjusted to combat on the frontier, was already in the tent when Amos and Dixon arrived.

"Gentlemen," Colonel Miles said as his palm up motion of his hand invited them to sit. Having no genuine confidence in the majority of his scouts, this was not a courtesy Miles often extended. Chapman and Dixon were the exceptions. Chapman and Dixon he not only trusted, he relied upon them and he had come to like them.

It was Amos Chapman's knowledge of the plains Indians that made him a clear exception. While he disapproved of Amos' choice to marry a Cheyenne woman and the fact that she was the daughter of Stone Calf would give him occasional pause, he knew Amos was a man to be trusted and his council to be valued.

Of Dixon, Miles had reached two firm conclusions. First, his words would be few and true. Dixon would tell you his truth even when he knew it was not what you wanted to hear. Second, in a firefight, he would like Dixon at his back. In Miles' mind Dixon was becoming a rare man, one for whom the Colonel had genuine admiration.

All seated, Colonel Miles, presenting the assumption that Captain Wyllys Lyman's supply was wandering somewhat lost, gave his directive. "Sergeant, I want that supply train located and re-directed. I want to overtake the Comanche before they can make the Palo Duro."

His eyes read the room, liking his reading he continued. "Sergeant, you may select three troopers to accompany you. Mr. Chapman and Mr. Dixon will provide guidance."

"Sergeant Woodall, when you have Captain Lyman back on his path, there are dispatches in need of delivery to Camp Supply. Select a trooper to accompany Mr. Dixon to Camp Supply with the dispatches."

Colonel Miles arose, turning his head against the breeze to re-light his cigar, then said, "Sergeant, boots and saddles within the hour. That's all."

He watched the three men depart the tent, knowing he had given all the instructions needed by the men he had selected for this mission.

133

As they walked away, Dixon said, "Know Lyman. He ain't lost."

"The Colonel knows. Dixon, he ain't sendin' ya cause he believes the Captain needs a talkin' to."

Thinking of Lyman, Amos said, "Ever notice a man losin' his top hair goes and grows big sideburns?"

Dixon shook his head, just a turn of the jaw to the right for him, in puzzlement at the relativity of Amos' comment, and then asked "Woodall?"

"He'll pick the best shots," Amos answered.

Dixon understood that to be relevant. He nodded.

The veteran Woodhall selected three of the best marksmen in the company for the mission, Privates John Harrington, Peter Roth and George Smith.

The party departed before mid-day, making quick time toward the Washita River basin.

Thirty-Seven

O n the afternoon of September 11, having tired of the siege of Lyman's supply train, about 120 hostiles departed to rejoin their families.

In the early morning of September 12, 1874, this same group of warriors intersected the path of the six-man patrol that Colonel Miles had sent to locate and re-direct Lyman with his badly needed supplies. Recognizing what appeared to be easy prey, the warriors quickly begin to move to encircle the patrol.

Dixon and Amos were a couple of lengths ahead of the soldiers when, without any movement of his upper torso, Amos asked, "Got 'em?"

"Got'em." Dixon acknowledged his awareness of the hostiles. Not that he'd missed the movement of a blade of grass since he left McLellan Creek. He seemed to glance around, then added, "Terrible open here."

"Yep," Amos allowed.

Within a minute, Sergeant Woodall eased up beside them. Again, Amos simply said, "Yep."

"A skirmish line when they come," Woodall said. The Sergeant did not have the slightest hint of a question in the phrasing.

Again, Amos' response was, "Yep." He added, "Can't be buffaloed."

"All about us anyways," Woodall said, then he eased back to his men.

The charge came. The patrol quickly grabbed rifles and their essentials bags as they dismounted. George Smith gathered the reins of all the mounts. The group's tight circle, a length apart, was formed. Woodall had selected well.

The first volley from the encircled band came in virtual unison. Then the reports of Chapman's Winchester and Dixon's Henry came more frequently than the troopers' Springfields would allow.

Early Private Smith, with his considerable strength, was able to hold the horses and release a pistol shot at the occasional hostile who made a thrust for the coveted horses.

Then a cartridge struck the Private squarely in the chest and George Smith dropped cold. In the din of the roar of battle, the already agitated horses broke free into the plains with several hostiles in pursuit.

Amos was closest and rose in an effort to grab the reins of at least one of the loose horses. A bullet struck and made his last lunges hobbled.

"God! God damn!" The words escaped through Amos' clenched teeth as the pain from the shell that tore into his left leg reached his brain. His jaw set firmer, forcing a deep guttural release of sound from between his teeth. He rolled over twice, his swearing scarcely audible, then brought his body stable. Stiffening, he secured his Winchester. Amos pulled himself into a position where Smith's body provided him with some protection.

He slammed a shell directly into the chamber to drop a hostile whose charge brought him within ten yards of Amos when he fell, then Amos started reloading his Winchester. The slight tremor the pain was bringing to his hand annoyed Amos.

"Ya 'live?" Dixon yelled.

The reply was a snort of disgust that Dixon had to ask. Mostly Amos was put out with himself for getting shot.

The horses breaking free brought a quick lull to the fight as the hostiles broke off the attack to pursue the valued animals. Dixon began to move toward what appeared to be an indention in the plains that he had spotted just before the attack began. After ten paces, he could make out the shape of a buffalo wallow, a deeper depression than most, and it just might provide enough shelter. It was for certain better than the open prairie.

Dixon had learned the lesson of Adobe Walls well. Any place that could be fortified would give the small patrol a chance at survival. In the pause, Dixon scrambled into the wallow, Roth and Harrington close on his heels. Without a word all three assumed a prone firing position at various edges of the wallow.

Dixon scanned the grass for Amos and Woodall. He spotted Amos moving in the grass.

"Waller, a waller," he yelled toward Amos as Woodall tumbled over him into the wallow. Woodall was quickly staring down the barrel of Dixon's newly acquired handgun.

"Lucky," Dixon muttered. Dixon knew had he been more experienced with the handgun, he might well have shot the already wounded Woodall. The Sergeant was just grateful in the wallow. It was deep enough to afford some protection, about twelve feet across and practically round.

Dixon turned his attention back to Amos' plight. Leaving Private Smith for dead, Amos was crawling, squirming and wiggling toward the wallow, dragging his completely shattered left leg along with him.

"Dig," was Dixon's only word to Woodall. The sternness of the single instruction transformed Woodall into Sergeant Z. T. Woodall, Company I, 6th U.S. Cavalry.

"Dig!" the Sergeant echoed in command voice.

Nothing about Adobe Walls was lost on Dixon. Woodall along with Harrington and Roth fanatically dug with rifle butts, knives and hands, loosening the dirt and debris, steeping the sides of the wallow, creating an outer rim.

The wallow itself provided the men with something of a natural firing pit, and their efforts made it more formidable. But it was still just an open hole on the prairie.

A voice in the Kiowa tongue carried over the grass. "Amos, you wiggle like a turtle."

Amos stopped, then yelled back toward the voice, "Lucky for me ya a poor shot, Fishinghawk. I'm a still wigglin'." While he had ridden many places with Fishinghawk, Amos couldn't believe the nature of the conversation, a good-humored taunting.

"Shake the grass, Amos. I shoot you."

"Dixon," Amos yelled.

"Got a sight," was the answer.

Amos slowly turned so that he could see up the slight incline, then reached out with his right arm as far as he could extend and shook a clump of grass. Fishinghawk's shot struck with a thud to Amos' right. Dixon got a clean sight on the smoke and fired.

"Amos, Dirty Hat shot my pony." Fishinghawk sounded exasperated.

"Shouldn't stand near 'em if you goin' shoot at folks," Amos shouted back. "Good thing Dirty Hat's a lousy shot."

Several chuckles arose from the grassy knoll.

"Amos, if you don't die today, we will hunt high in the Red country when it gets cooler."

"Be lookin' to it."

Dixon, taking advantage of the conversational distraction, quickly crawled the fifteen yards from the wallow to Amos' side. No words passed, but Amos' grip on Dixon's shoulder expressed the considerable appreciation Amos felt for the assistance he was about to receive. Dixon drug the wiggling Amos into the wallow.

As the pair tumbled into the depression, Dixon saw the bone of Amos' femur sticking through the hole in his pants around the blood-soaked knee.

"Amos, ya leg's blowed all to hell," Dixon muttered.

"Hadn't noticed," was Amos' sarcastic reply.

Again, Dixon's smile just tightened the lips, barely raising the corners of his mouth, and he shook his head. Dixon liked this man.

"Ya could help," Amos said as he was removing his shirt and cutting the sleeves out to make a bandage for his badly shattering leg. As Dixon moved to help, he realized Amos' lower leg was scarcely attached to his thigh, in truth just a limp appendage dangling from his body. John Harrington came to Amos' assistance. Using Amos' shirt to compress the wound, he used his own leather braces for strapping.

Amos pulled himself to the edge of the wallow and began to dig. Another thrust came toward Sergeant Woodall's area just as Chapman had scratched himself a position near Woodall. Roth and Harrington moved to support Sergeant Woodall. The fire from the four was so efficient and lethal that this would be the last direct frontal thrust toward the wallow.

However, the one hostile who made it within ten yards of the men put a clean shot into Private Harrington's shoulder before Roth, using his revolver at the close distance, shot the charging warrior dead.

The hostiles had withdrawn beyond any line of sight, as stories of the long shot at the place of the rotting walls were rampant and exaggerated among the Comanche and Kiowa on the Llano.

With three of their surviving party now wounded, Sergeant Woodall concurred with Dixon and Chapman's assessment. They needed the water and ammunition that lay in the grass with George Smith.

"Me," was the extent of Roth's volunteer statement. With Dixon and Chapman poised to provide covering fire if needed, Private Peter Roth disappeared into the grass.

Shortly, Roth tumbled back into the wallow carrying Smith's Springfield, pistol, cartridge belt and water bag. The excited Roth, his rapid-fire words now mostly his native German, conveyed little other than his blend of trepidation and amazement. As he became more agitated with his attempts to communicate, he began to rise from his knees. A bullet whistled as a clear target presented itself.

Woodall grabbed Roth by the belt and pulled him down to a seated position.

"Private!" Woodall's bark had the sobering effect of a firm slap. "Report in English, Private."

Roth's breathing leveled, but a thick German accent still veiled his words. "By damn, Sergeant, he's alive. Can't see how but he's breathin'." Roth's voice became a murmur offering a muted testament to his own disbelief.

"Who's alive, Soldier?" Sergeant Z. T. Woodall asked while retaining the voice of authority to allow Roth to further calm.

Finding his English voice again, Roth replied, "Trooper Smith, Sergeant."

"God, be blessed." Chapman inserted. "He done filled ole Georgie boy full a' girt." Amos continued, "Gotta get that boy ta home."

"Gotta be shot up, best with friends." Amos patted his own blood-soaked leg.

"Scout, I'd not consider leaving a man I could get to," Woodall barked.

"Z.T., I meant no such offense," Amos explained.

Woodall's nod toward Amos was accepting and understanding, then he said, "Volunteers."

"Roth, be us," was Dixon's stoic conclusion. Although not yet completely convinced that it was not George's ghost that laid in the grass, Roth agreed.

Peter Roth and Billy Dixon crawled over the edge of the wallow and quickly disappeared into the tall grass. Almost uneventfully, the pair reeled in their barely breathing but still somewhat conscious comrade. Private George Smith was brought into the relative safety of the wallow.

Smith blinked his almost set eyes and attempted to nod when Sergeant Woodall said, "Trooper, glad ya here."

The Kiowa again attacked, this time circling the wallow rather than risking another direct attack. The circling attack would be continuous, as a warrior would be shot or tired of shooting at the small targets in the wallow would simply leave the circle and another would soon take his place. But the threat to the men in wallow was constant.

A situational awareness crept into the consciousness of the mortally wounded George Smith. George tried to reach for his Springfield, but his grasp failed him. He had no feeling in his arms or hands.

As if realizing the circumstances with a perspective perhaps only a dying man, a dying soldier, can obtain, George pressed his heels into the dirt and clay of the wallow and with a show of incredible determination began the slow, arduous process of forcing his limbs and torso up the side of the wallow, finally bringing himself into a sitting but fully exposed position against the bank of the wallow.

George fought with his comrades in the only way available to him. He became a visible target drawing hostile fire.

Suddenly, several of the Kiowa stopped their ponies and drew dead aim on the wallow. Their shots flew into the wallow and seemed to whistle off Dixon and Amos' heads. As they pulled their heads to safety and turned, they saw what had drawn the Kiowa fire.

George had drawn the Kiowa fire away from his comrades and provided them with targets of opportunity.

"Now," Dixon yelled in possibly the loudest voice he had ever used.

Dixon, Amos and Woodall struck at the available Kiowa targets George had provided them, killing eight of the hostiles who made the fatal mistake of stopping their ponies for a clear shot at Private George Smith before Roth and Harrington could pull Smith back below the line of fire.

Sergeant Woodall crawled to George Smith, looked squarely into his eyes, and in as military a voice as he could muster, said, "Private Smith, well done." He paused, unable to suppress the raw humanity of emotions, and said "Georgie, ya a hell of a soldier."

If Smith could have displayed his pleasure at his Sergeant's approval, he would have, but consciousness had again left him.

Woodall loosened his kerchief from his neck, dampened it with a small amount of precious water and with the gentlest of touches wiped the dust from the corners of George's mouth, then laid the kerchief on his forehead.

Thirty-Eight

$\mathcal{N}$ ow in the mid-afternoon heat, the intensity of the Kiowa attack had slackened. The west Texas sun and the limited water supply were taking their toll on the men barricaded in the wallow.

Dixon nudged Amos as the breeze freshened from the northwest, bending the grass and carrying a hint of cooling moisture. Dixon interlocked his fingers and stared into the darkening sky.

And then as if by divine intervention, the storm clouds that the defenders of the wallow had been watching since noon rolled over the wallow, bringing a premature darkness. The sky was lit by fierce bolts of lightning unleashed from the clouds, followed by crashing rolls of thunder that seemed to shake the grass around the wallow. Then, beginning with large cold droplets and becoming stinging wind-driven torrents, the rain arrived.

The five scrambled to make places for the water to collect inside the wallow. And puddle it did, and containers while not filled held more water than they had.

Then the bitter cold air that had propelled the storm arrived.

Amos shivered, then he became thoughtful, then he became hopeful. "Dixon, my bet's them Kiowa was headed home and stumbled on us. 'Ready got our horses. Know Fishinghawk ain't gonna get cold and wet just to kill us."

As Dixon was agreeing, another wave of rain arrived, a cold misty rain that would cling to a man, chill him to his very bones.

"Shoulda kept a buffalo chip dry," Amos somewhat wishfully observed.

"Couldn't keep us dry," Sergeant Woodall entered the discussion.

"See what mornin' brings," Dixon concluded.

"Puttin' Georgie between Roth and Harrington. Keep him a little warmer," Woodall advised.

As the deep darkness of the heavily overcast night punctuated with intermittent rain began to settle fully over the wallow, Dixon, certainly the least injured of the party, eased over the rim of the wallow and was instantly out of sight. At first crawling, and then crouching, he began to reconnoiter the area.

By Woodall's pocket watch just short of an hour later, he returned still somewhat crouched, but the pace of his movement told Amos and Woodall that they were now alone on the prairie.

Dixon eased by into the wallow, lost his balance in the mud on the edge, but Roth reached up and steadied him.

"Nary sight, sound or sign," Dixon reported, confirming what Amos and the Sergeant had surmised by the cautious but casual manner of his movement back to the wallow.

Dixon eased in next to Amos.

"Just might make it back to Mary," Amos allowed.

"Like the smell of the grass after a rain," was Dixon's reply.

The six men burrowed in, the five quite protective of their companion, George Smith. They huddled together and would try to survive the night.

Private George Smith, Company M, 6th United States Calvary, died between his protective fellow Troopers during the early morning hours of September 13, 1874. On that cold, rainy night, Private John Harrington, Company H, 6th United States Calvary, used his own shirt to cover the face of his fallen friend.

The morning broke clear and crisp. The Kiowa had abandoned the fight and were likely making their way toward their winter camps.

But the small band of survivors had no mounts, and all save Dixon were so severely wounded that they could not leave the wallow.

Amos looked directly at Dixon and said, "Somebody gotta go."

The response was a simple, "Yep."

After this extremely brief conference, Dixon, most closely resembling an able-bodied individual so to speak, volunteered to attempt to locate assistance for the party. He took his almost depleted essentials bag and left the wallow.

Dixon's pace was dictated more by his discomfort and his sheer exhaustion than by his skills. But sitting for an occasional rest was a luxury he was reluctant to permit himself. During the only break he allowed himself, he wound up with a sleeve full of sand burrs. Surprised by his own weakness, he had stumbled into the burrs in his effort to get up.

Then, the biting flies seem to find him.

Within an hour, he found the military trail. He now moved with a haste tempered only by his awareness that any Comanche worth his salt could find the trail easily and would be enticed by a target of opportunity such as he presented.

As Dixon's body tired, his raw determination increased in proportion. This sheer force of will would sustain the pace of his trek, the steely focus of eyes sustaining his hyper-alert vigil for friend or foe.

By noon, he spotted a column on the military trail. The reasonably orderly movement suggested they were in fact Calvary. Regardless, Dixon settled himself on the hillside, retrieved his binoculars from his essentials bag and checked the column. Satisfied, he fired his sidearm into the air. He saw two outriders moving quickly toward him.

Dixon laid back into the slope of the rise, waved a fly from his neck and began to pick the remaining sand burrs from his sleeve.

Thirty-Nine

*D*ixon had intercepted units of the 8th Cavalry from the New Mexico Territory under the command of Major William Price.

Price, his surgeon and 25 troopers accompanied Dixon back to the wallow. Unfortunately, by the time of their arrival one of the now sun-scorched and severely dehydrated occupants of the wallow was experiencing the onset of delusions and hallucinations, thinking the approaching column was the Kiowa returning, and he shot the horse from under the one of the surgeon's assistants, enraging the surgeon.

Almost unbelievably, the surgeon gave the wounded men only the most basic of care. Major Price refused to leave the scout party even ammunition, food or blankets, much less reinforcements. However, some of his troopers, many of those in the Troop who were outraged at the conduct of their Major and his surgeon, did leave the survivors water, hardtack and dried beef.

Dixon gathered buffalo chips, flaking off an adequate number of dry materials to start a fire in middle of the wallow. The damp chips quickly dried in the afternoon sun and the unvarying breeze.

Major Price did send a galloper to find Colonel Miles on McMillan Creek.

Just after midnight on September 14, the recovery party with a surgeon and an ambulance from General Miles' staff arrived at the wallow, bringing the desperately needed medical attention and food.

It was only now that Private George Smith was carefully wrapped in a military blanket and taken to the center of wallow. Encircled by his wounded companions and every member of the recovery party, under the supervision of his badly wounded Sergeant, George Smith was buried on the plains of West Texas near the Wichita River with as close to full honors as the conditions allowed.

The remaining five were taken by military ambulance to Camp Supply in the Indian Territory for further treatment. Once in the hospital, Amos Chapman's severely damaged left leg was amputated.

Sergeant Zachariah T. Woodall, Sergeant, Company I, 6th United States Calvary, Private Peter Roth, Company A, 6th United States Calvary, Private John Harrington, Company H, 6th United States Calvary, Private George Smith (Posthumously), Company M, 6th United States Calvary, Scout Amos Chapman and Scout William Dixon were awarded the Congressional Medal of Honor for gallantry action on the Wichita River on 12 September 1874.

Billy Dixon was presented his Medal of Honor by Colonel Nelson Miles at Carson Creek, very near the site of Adobe Walls.

Dixon was recorded as having been involved in the rescue of the Germaine Sisters on McCellan Creek on November 8, 1874, less than two months after the Fight at Buffalo Wallow. He remained a scout for the United States Calvary until 1883.

John Harrington and Zachariah Woodall continued their military careers.

In a Calvary in which the large majority of its leadership ardently clung to the axiom "Mount and ride to the sound of the guns", his decision at Buffalo Wallow was the pivotal point in the military career of Major William R. Price. He was severely censured for his failure to provide assistance to the survivors. This inglorious act remained the most memorable deed of his military career.

Along Life's Paths

Amos Chapman (1839-1925) After his recovery, he was fitted with an artificial leg. Over the following years he served as an interpreter for the United States Government. He was married to Mary Longneck and was active advocate for his father-in-law, the Cheyenne Chief Stone Calf. He was effective mediator in a number of disputes between feuding cattleman.

Eventually, he and his wife operated a ranch near Seiling, Oklahoma. Despite having a reasonably comfortable ranch home, the Chapmans are said to have often spent their nights sleeping under the open sky.

He was injured in a wagon accident and he died some days later on July 18, 1925.

Amos and Mary Chapman are buried in Brumfield Cemetery just north of Seiling, Oklahoma.

William "Billy" Dixon (1850-1913) Billy Dixon retained his affiliation with United States Calvary until 1883 and never returned to the buffalo trade. He filed a homestead and lived on or near the site of Adobe Walls. Over the coming years in addition to farming, he would serve Hutchinson County, Texas, in a number of government positions ranging from Postmaster to Sheriff to Justice of the Peace.

He married Olive King in October of 1894. It is said that for the next several years, she would be the only white woman residing in Hutchinson County. They had seven children.

In 1902, they moved into a small community nearby for the education of their children. Dixon felt confined by even small-town life, and in 1906 he filed a homestead in Oklahoma Territory.

In an effort to alleviate what had become virtual abject poverty, Olive King Dixon wrote an account of Dixon's life. While many viewed it as a cross between the truth and a dime novel, it appears to have been written with the very best of intents. It would be published a year after his death.

William "Billy" Dixon died on March 9, 1913, of pneumonia, in poverty but on his homestead in the less confining regions of the Oklahoma panhandle.

With the final expenses paid by his Masonic brothers (The Hutchinson County, Texas, Masonic Lodge is named in his honor), an original burial was conducted near his homestead.

On June 27, 1929, he was re-interred at the site of Adobe Walls.

Elder, Kate (Mary Katherine Horony Cummings) (1850-1940) Arriving in Fort Griffin, Texas, she began her long-time relationship with the legendary western figure John Henry "Doc" Holliday. Their path took her through a variety of Colorado mining towns, to Las Vegas, New Mexico, then into the Arizona Territory, moving from Prescott to Globe and to Tombstone.

Following the events at the OK Corral in Tombstone (1881) and the vendetta, she went to Redstone, Colorado, near Glenwood Springs, where Holliday was seeking treatment in the "curative sulfur waters" found in the springs. Holliday died in November of 1887.

In 1890, Kate married George Cummings in Aspen, Colorado. The marriage to the alcoholic, abusive Cummings was short-lived. Kate returned to Arizona.

Kate died on November 6, 1940, at the age of 89 while residing the Arizona Pioneers' Home in Prescott, Arizona. She is buried under the name of Mary K. Cummings at The Arizona Pioneer Home Cemetery, Prescott, Arizona.

William Barclay "Bat" Masterson (1855-1921) In 1876, Wyatt Earp hired him as a Deputy City Marshall in Dodge City, Kansas. In 1877, he became the Sheriff of Ford County while his brother, Ed, was the Marshal of Dodge City. He lost his bid for re-election in 1879.

During the next 10 years, he plied the gambling skills he had acquired in Sweetwater in mining communities, including

Tombstone, Arizona, Trinidad, and Creed, Colorado. He served briefly as the town marshal in the latter two towns.

Masterson then took up residence in Denver, Colorado, bought the Palace Variety Theatre and in 1891 married Emma Walters, an aspiring actress. Masterson also wrote a weekly sports column for a Denver newspaper.

While he primarily was a gambler, he opened the Olympic Athletic Club begin to actively promote prize fights, the most memorable of which was an 1896 $10,000 Heavyweight Championship fight between Fitzsimmons and Mahler scheduled for El Paso, Texas, despite the fact that prize fighting was illegal in Texas. Dodging the Texas Rangers, the fight was ultimately held 100 yards into Mexico, south of Langtry, Texas, under the guidance of Judge Roy Bean.

He moved to New York City in 1902.

President Theodore Roosevelt appointed Masterson the United States Deputy Marshall in the Southern District of New York. He stayed in this position from 1905 to 1909.

In 1907, while serving as United States Deputy Marshall, he took a job as a sports columnist for the New York Morning Telegraph.

In his office at the New York Morning Telegraph on October 25, 1921, Bat Masterson slumped over his typewriter in the midst of writing his column and died of a heart attack.

He is buried in Woodlawn Cemetery in the Bronx, New York.

"Every dog, we are told, has his day, unless there are more dogs than days"
– William Barclay Masterson.

"There are those who argue that everything breaks even in this old dump of a world of ours. I suppose these ginks who argue that way hold that because the rich man gets ice in the summer and the poor man gets it in the winter, things are breaking even for both. Maybe so, but I'll swear I can't see it that way."
– William Barclay Masterson

Olds, Hannah (Mrs. William) Hannah Olds departed Adobe Walls promptly after the fight of 1874. She was met in Dodge City, Kansas, by her close friend Carrie (Mrs. Charles) Rath. After spending some time with the Raths, she is said to have returned to her eastern roots and vanished from western lore.

Quanah Parker (1850-1911)

"Not only did Quanah pass within the span of a single lifetime from a Stone Age warrior to a statesman in the age of the Industrial Revolution, but he accepted the challenge and responsibility of leading the whole Comanche tribe on the difficult road toward their new existence."

The Last Comanche Chief: The Life and Times of Quanah Parker.

– Bill Neeley (Biographer and Author)

Guided by his vision of an eagle gliding toward Fort Sill and his trust in Jacob J. Sturm, the representative of Colonel Ranald S. Mackenzie, the war-weary Quanah surrendered on June 2, 1875, at Fort Sill, Indian Territory (Near Lawton, Oklahoma).

Taking his mother's last name, Quanah Parker became an ardent advocate of an enculturation of the Comanche while preserving significant elements of Nermernuh culture and traditions. The most controversial of these practices being the continued use of peyote as an integral part of religion, spreading Christian peyotism, and sustaining polygamy as the base of the family system.

Conversely, he was equally adamant about the establishment of an educational system for the Nermernuh, using English as the basic language and classes taught by conventionally educated white teachers. He believed Indian teachers would not speak the type nor the quantity of English the Comanche children needed to learn.

In general, he believed adopting the majority of the "white ways" would in due course provide the greatest benefit to his people. Quanah learned to read and came to be fluent in three languages, English, Comanche, and Spanish.

Quanah understood how to make the lease agreement system benefit his people. He strongly encouraged ranching, an activity he saw as consistent with the Comanche temperament, and farming to a lesser degree. Many of his people did become very successful ranchers.

While most historians agree that greed was not a primary motivator for Quanah, he did acquire significant wealth as a result of his political and business transactions with the "white world". His friends in this world would range from rancher Charles Goodnight to President Theodore Roosevelt.

His boyhood friend, Howeah, became his most vigorous and outspoken political opponent, opposing any decision to "travel the white man's road" often referring to Quanah's "half-white blood".

Weakeah remained his favorite wife until her death. He had children by his other wives.

Quanah did remove his mother's remains from the cemetery in Anderson County, Texas. He first moved her to the Post Oak Cemetery in Cache, Oklahoma. Only three months before Quanah's death, she was re-interred at Chief's Knoll in the Fort Sill Military Cemetery near Lawton, Oklahoma. Two weeks before his death, he saw the monument he so desired for her placed upon her grave.

Quanah Parker died on February 23, 1911, and was buried next to his mother.

Military Survivors of the Fight at Buffalo Wallow

Harrington, John (1848-1905) Recipient of the Medal of Honor for his action at Buffalo Wallow. He remained on active military duty until 1898. He is buried in the National Cemetery in San Antonio, Texas.

Roth, Peter Paul (Unknown) Recipient of the Medal of Honor for his action at Buffalo Wallow. He was born in Wurtlemberg,

Germany, enlisted in the military in Brooklyn, New York, and is buried in his native Germany.

Woodall, Zachariah T. (1850-1899) Recipient of the Medal of Honor for his action at Buffalo Wallow. He remained on active military duty until near the time of his death. He is buried in Arlington National Cemetery.

Recommendation Letter of Nelson A. Miles
In the matter of the Fight at Buffalo Wallow

Adjutant General, U.S. Army

General: – I deem it but a duty to brave men and faithful soldiers, to bring to the notice of the highest military authority an instance of indomitable courage, skill and true heroism on the part of a detachment from this command, with the request that the actors be rewarded, and their faithfulness and bravery recognized by pensions, medals of honor, or in such way as may be deemed fitting.

On the night of 10th instant a party consisting of Sergeant Z.T. Woodall, Troop I; Privates Peter Roth, Troop A; John Harrington, Troop H; and George W. Smith, Troop M, 6th Cavalry; Scouts Amos Chapman and William Dixon, were sent as bearers of dispatches from the camp of this command on McLellan Creek, Texas to Camp Supply, Indian Territory. At six a.m., on the 12th, when approaching Washita River, they were met and surrounded by a band of 125 Kiowas and Comanches, who had recently left their agency, and at the first attack all were struck, Private Smith mortally, and all the others severely wounded.

Although enclosed on all sides, and by overwhelming numbers, one of them succeeded, while they were under a severe fire at short range, and while the others with their rifles were keeping the Indians at bay, in digging with his knife and hands a slight cover. After this had been secured they placed themselves within it, the wounded walking with brave and painful efforts, and Private Smith, though he had received a mortal wound, sitting upright in the trench to conceal the crippled condition of their party from the Indians.

From early morning till dark, outnumbered twenty-five to one, under an almost constant fire, and at such short range that they sometimes used their pistols, retaining the last charge to prevent capture and torture, this little party of five defended their lives and the person of their dying comrade, without food and their only drink the rain water that collected in a pool, mingled with their own blood. There is no doubt but that they killed more than double their number, besides those that were wounded. The Indians abandoned the attack at dark on the 12th.

The exposure and the distance from the command, which were necessary incidents of their duty, were such that for thirty-six hours from the first attack their condition could not be known, and not till midnight of the 13th could they receive medical attendance or food; exposed during this time to an incessant cold storm. Sergeant Woodall, Private Harrington, and Scout Chapman were seriously wounded; Private Roth and Scout Dixon were struck but not disabled.

The simple recital of their deeds and the mention of the odds against which they fought, how the wounded defended the dying, and the dying aided the wounded by exposure to fresh would after the power of action was gone, they alone present a scene a cool courage, heroism and self-sacrifice, which duty as well as inclination prompts us to recognize, but which we cannot fitly honor.

(Signed) N. A. Miles
Brevet Major-General

As cited in:
From Yorktown To Santiago
With the Sixth U.S. Cavalry
By Lieutenant-Colonel W. H. Carter
The Lord Baltimore Press
Baltimore, Maryland
1900

www.ingramcontent.com/pod-product-compliance
Lightning Source LLC
Chambersburg PA
CBHW020131180626
46810CB00004B/1499